Folded dreams

A lieutenant Beaudry novel

MEZZO PUBLICATIONS

Montreal Canada

ISBN: 0993713106
ISBN-13: 978-0-9937131-0-1

Cover art by Trzah's Book Covers

DEDICATION

For my mother who gave our family the love of reading

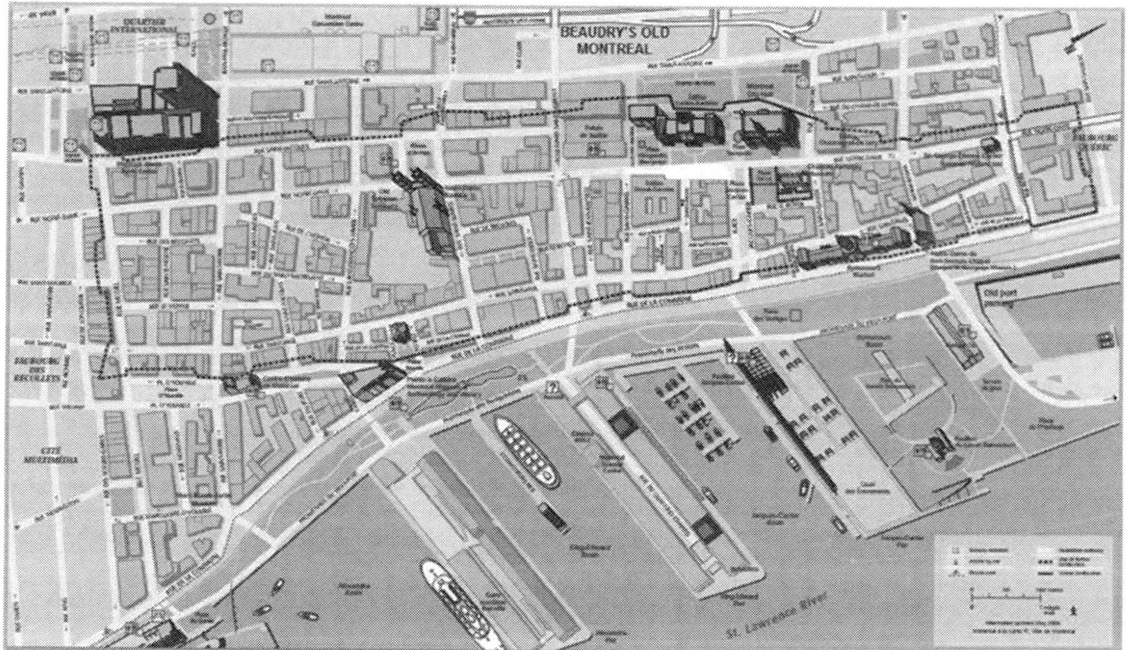
BEAUDRY'S OLD
MONTREAL
St. Lawrence River

ACKNOWLEDGMENTS

My grateful appreciation to Jax Franklin and all the other reviewers on The Next Big Writer, for their insights, corrections, and kind support.

Also, deepest thanks go to fellow author Don P. Chambers for graciously reading from the first chapter to the last and for his many insightful suggestions.

A debt of gratitude to my editor Michael Carr who has taught me so much.

April is the cruellest month, breeding
Lilacs out of the dead land, mixing
Memory and desire, stirring
Dull roots with spring rain.

~T.S. Eliot

ONE

In the mood to do nothing today, I was enjoying the fresh April breeze and that first sip of coffee. From the weathered rocking chair on my third-floor balcony, I could see the cobblestone lanes of Old Montreal, two blocks south. I could also see my boss driving up. I scratched my three-day beard. Now what?

The captain parked in front of my house, bounded out of his car, and marched up the steps.

I hadn't spoken to him since the day, some six months ago, that he kicked me out of his office. In a hostage situation gone wrong, I had shot some bad guys, I had been a bit fast on the trigger and my excessive enthusiasm earned me an indefinite suspension.

When Internal Affairs asked me why I had shot two bank robbers dead and wounded a third, I told them I was rusty because I hadn't been to the range lately. They hadn't appreciated my humor—gave me the choice of counseling or the suspension.

When the doorbell rang, I walked back into the hallway and hit the intercom. "There's nobody home but the cat."

"Go tell Robert I need to talk to him now."

Reluctantly, I buzzed the door open. "Come on up, Jean."

As always, and in keeping with his by-the-book management style, Jean O'Neil was impeccably turned out. A slim six feet six, he stood straight as a pool shark's cue, his mustache trimmed and every bristle of his salt-and-pepper brush cut in precise formation. But for the crooked nose and the furrows on each side of his mouth, he could have been moderately handsome.

We had worked together for the past eight years, but my loose interpretation of the rule book often put us at odds. Jean would have made a good politician—it wasn't easy to get a solid yes or a final no out of him, and his instructions were often gray. It left me enough wiggle room to get myself in trouble.

He looked around the room. "Holy crap! I like what you did to your loft: exposed brick, built-in bookcases, new skylight—very nice. You didn't waste your vacation time."

"Suspension, not vacation," I said.

Jean sat down on the piano bench. "Suspension with pay—same thing."

"Doesn't leave quite the same taste."

"Speaking of taste, you going to offer me a coffee?"

Heading to the Breville percolator in the kitchen, I said over my shoulder, "You here at ten to seven in the morning for coffee, or decorating tips?"

I walked back in with my hard-to-hold Disney mug filled to the brim. Jean grabbed it by both of Mickey's ears and took a careful sip. "I came to find out if you're back in shape."

"I'm into tai chi—helps with flexibility."

Jean tilted his head and tapped his index finger on his forehead. "After Colleen's funeral, you walked around in a daze for weeks. I wasn't sure if you were about to go over the edge."

"My ex-wife killed herself, and I still can't put a reason to it. So maybe I was introspective for a couple of days. What did you expect?"

"You think that you're Superman, but you're not. Your head was messed up; you needed some time off. We gave it to you."

I tuned to Jean, my hand on my heart. "I have fought the feelings and emotions inside that fills and empties me, like a fast rolling tide. There are moments of pain, of sorrow and hate, leaving me to ponder many hours of late."

He gave me a furtive smile, the caterpillar under his nose twisting into an ill-formed crescent. "I can see you've read all the books on your shelves. You always come up with some weird little quote."

"That was from 'One Last Kiss,' by Marty Pijanowski," I said. "I guarantee you, I'm back to my abnormal self. I'm so focused, I can see that one of your sideburns is a full thirty-second of an inch lower than the other. Of course, it works out okay since that ear's lower, too."

"Now, *there's* the smart-assed cop I know," Jean said.

"So, is my suspension lifted or not?"

He stood up, fished a wallet-size leather case out of his raincoat, and handed me my badge. "Robert, your vacation is *fini,* and I'm giving you a new partner."

"You know I work alone," I said.

"I can't have you running loose again. You have to learn to work on a team. My niece, Patricia, just transferred from Fraud to Homicide. She needs a mentor."

"I look like a babysitter?"

"She's far from a baby, and you have the street smarts to keep her out of trouble. More importantly, she's strong willed, with enough sense of humor to put up with you."

I looked at him over the rim of my cup and slurped my coffee. "Your office at nine tomorrow?" I said.

"Wrong. You were back on the job twenty minutes ago. There's a dead woman folded into the trunk of a BMW in the Old Port parking lot, four blocks from here. You've got fifteen minutes to shave and make yourself presentable. I'll drive. We'll meet my niece at the scene."

I showered and shaved in record time, Jean leaned on the bedroom doorjamb while I finished dressing.

My cat strolled out of the bathroom and passed between us, trailing a five-foot toilet-paper streamer from his mouth.

"You teach him that trick?" Jean said.

"Nah, just more daily mischief. That cat is a total nutcase. That's why I named him 'Crackers.' Now he'll bring it to the living room, where he'll shred it into tiny bits. I inherited a seriously troubled feline."

As the last foot of toilet paper disappeared down the hall, Jean said, "Speaking of trouble, you won't have Lorne Trehearne breathing down your neck anymore. He's out of Internal Affairs and working directly for the mayor. Now all you have to worry about is me personally gutting you with an apple corer if you get my favorite niece hurt."

"So, Lord Lorne's working for the mayor. In this administration, brown-nosing pays off."

Jean didn't rebut my comment as he followed me to the hall closet. Using my house key to unlock the metal gun box on the closet shelf, I grabbed my holster, spare piece, and a loaded extra magazine. Jean gave me a slit-eyed look as I cycled a round into the chamber and flipped the safety up, then put on my shoulder rig.

"Weren't you supposed to turn in your weapon?"

"I did. This is my spare. I can't go out on a case unarmed. I'd feel naked."

The captain gave an impatient sigh. "Beaudry, just try and solve the case without shooting anyone. I may not be able to go to bat for you next time—City Hall's not in the mood for another shoot-out. You've been warned: next time, no suspension. It'll be a one-way ticket off the job."

I put on my leather jacket, and we headed for the door. On the way out, I took a last look at my apartment. For the past few years, I had lived the James Dean quote: "Dream as if you'll live forever, live as if you'll die today." In my line of work, maybe I'd be back tonight, maybe not. At this point in my life, I wasn't sure how much I cared.

TWO

"The Old Port" is a misnomer; it's actually new. It's a renovated part of Old Montreal. The nineteenth-century waterfront dock warehouses now house museums, a science center, an IMAX theater, and trendy restaurants. Boutiques and art galleries make up the rest of the neighborhood. Walking down the cobblestone streets, if you don't look at what's in the stores, it feels like you've time-traveled back to the Paris of a century ago. As if to emphasize this, a single horse-drawn carriage passed us, going the opposite direction. It was early April, and the tourist season had yet to blossom. Few people were at the Old Port.

The Beamer was at the far end of the parking lot, cordoned off with yellow police tape and surrounded by four patrol cars and a shiny new tech-squad truck. The rest of the parking spaces were empty, outlined by oil stains and tire tracks in dirty salt and sand—the gritty remnants of winter.

As we walked up to the BMW, a slim, spike-haired twenty-something crime-scene officer came around the car. "Lieutenant Beaudry! You're back," he said.

His toothy smile brought back the memory of working a particularly gruesome crime scene with him a year ago. I was glad to see him here. The kid was a true genius in the lab, with a knack for finding the one hidden link that glued the evidence together. His testimony often prompted defense attorneys to throw in the towel and ask for a deal, while the crown prosecutors smiled like Cheshire cats.

I wanted to tell him I was glad to see him, but before I could comment, Jean O'Neil spoke. I could see by the frown lines on his forehead that something was worrying him. He nodded toward both of us. "Sergeant Dobson, Beaudry's got lead on this one. Bring him up to speed. I have to be back downtown. Robert, walk me to my car; I want to talk to you."

We spoke as I followed Jean to his car. "Okay, boss, what's with the frowny face? I haven't so much as *thought* of shooting anyone yet."

"Watch out for your new partner. She's a bit of a wild Irish girl. The color of her hair may give you a hint of her temper, but be advised, her bite's worse than her bark."

I walked back and said to Dobson, "Glad to see you again. What have you CSI whiz kids got so far?"

Dobson pointed into the open car trunk. The body of a woman lay as if sleeping on her right side, her legs tucked in a crouch. Both hands were out in front, as if pushing something invisible away from her. As I bent down to look closer, Dobson said, "Don't touch anything. We haven't finished sweeping yet."

Her long auburn hair reflected the early morning sun. I took a step to the right and looked down at the victim. Her skin shone with the waxy look of death, but her oval face was perfect and unblemished. She had full lips and a cute, pert nose.

"She looks peacefully asleep, it's the bullet hole behind her left ear that gives it away," I said.

"Yeah, right, Lieutenant."

"So, where are we with this?" I said.

"Eh, there are only a few drops of blood on the carpet. She was probably killed somewhere else, then placed in the trunk. She must have died some four or five hours ago at the outside. Rigor mortis is only partial. The trunk may have helped keep the body warm."

I nodded. Encouraged, Dobson continued.

"There's no license plate on the car, and we didn't find a purse, registration, or insurance papers. There's a dent on the rear bumper and the trunk; that's why it doesn't close. The rest of the car is immaculate. It's been wiped clean. We probably won't get prints, but we'll dust anyhow, just in case we get lucky. The body has two small-caliber wounds: the one you saw behind the left ear, and another just left of center in her chest. We'll have more from the autopsy."

Shaking my head, I said, "What a waste! She was a beautiful woman. Somebody's wife or girlfriend, somebody's mother, maybe. This mess will affect a bunch of people. I'm sure a lot of future hopes and dreams got folded up in that trunk with her."

"Eh, I see a dead body; you see folded dreams. Your mental camera catches things from a little different angle than most people's. Welcome back, Lieutenant. We were starting to get bored down in the lab."

I moved back from the car, and Dobson stuck his hand out. We shook, and he did a sudden sidestep, staring down the side street behind me. Someone at the entrance of the parking lot was cursing like a Canadian hockey coach on a losing streak.

"You're missing a good show," Dobson said. "A redhead just tried to step over the warning tape. It snapped up between her legs and pushed up her skirt."

As I turned toward the commotion, she slapped down at the offending tape and broke it. In the wind, the long end slithered around on the ground like a riled snake.

"That must be my new partner," I said with a grin.

She made her way toward us, avoiding the oily puddles and mounds of dirt. She was well dressed and color coordinated in a tight gray skirt and a black leather jacket over a maroon sweater. Her gold badge hung just below a patterned gray scarf , one end artfully draped over her right breast.

Admiring her, I remembered a Jack Benny quote: "Give me golf clubs, fresh air, and a beautiful partner, and you can keep the clubs and the fresh air."

She read Dobson's name tag. "Good morning, Sergeant Dobson. I'm Patricia O'Neil, the big guy's partner."

Dobson's eyes lit up. I stuck my hand out. "I guess that makes me the big guy."

Pat's grip felt as firm as the rest of her looked. She gave me a smile that would melt titanium.

"Sorry, Lieutenant Beaudry. The captain told me to look for a walking refrigerator of a man."

I gave her my best grin. "Years of serious weightlifting have given me my manly wide shoulders and young-Schwarzenegger physique."

Dobson snickered when Pat said, "Like Arnold in his movies, I understand that you also shoot holes in things."

"Hearsay and innuendo—I'm a teddy bear," I said.

She turned and bent over the corpse in the trunk. Dobson, appreciating the view, didn't admonish her for getting too close.

"I see your tech team has bagged her hands," she said to Dobson.

"She may have scratched her attacker or molester," he replied. I'll check her nails at the autopsy."

"With all due respect to ya Dobson, her clothes tell us she wasn't molested," Pat said. "There's a spot of blood on her chest, but no dirt, no rips or popped buttons on her blouse. Her skirt isn't twisted, the zipper is in line with her spine, and everything looks intact. I'd say there was no malarkey just a the kill. From the placing of her, I'd say it took two people to pick her up and deposit her carefully in the trunk."

"I just told the lieutenant she was probably killed somewhere else, then placed in the trunk."

"The poor craiter," Pat said. "It's a real shame. She was a beek and a half, her hair smells freshly washed, and she's all dolled up and wearing 'going out' makeup."

"Beek?" I said.

"Sorry, Lieutenant Bear, it's Irish slang. She was a real looker.

She bent and turned down the victim's jacket collar. Dobson didn't say a word.

"She wasn't skint; she had money. Look at this label: Veronica Beard with the matching skirt. Probably cost a thousand plus. The Christian Louboutin shoes—that's another thousand—and her blouse is probably from some other poufy designer with stratospheric price points."

My new partner was good-looking, professional in her observations, and showed a sense of humor. I let her get away with the "Lieutenant Bear" comment.

"What else do you deduce, Miss Sherlock?" I said.

"A shot to the heart with a twenty-two, followed by a coup de grâce to the head, isn't simple murder. It's a bloody execution. I'd be gobsmacked if it wasn't a professional hit."

"Oookay, we're on the same page. The car's wiped clean, purse gone, no ID. Apart from a fresh dent on the rear bumper and trunk, there's not much evidence left for us. A professional hit man will be erasing his tracks within hours."

I turned to Dobson. "I need everything in high gear. No nine-to-five on this, and no stopping for paperwork."

As I spoke, a beat officer walked up behind us.

"Lieutenant," the patrolman said, "I have the vagrant who found the victim earlier this morning. He told us the trunk was partially open, so he peeked in."

"So where is he? What's with the funny grin?" I asked.

He pointed to the end of the parking lot. "My partner has him standing behind our unit. It's car fourteen, over to the left. Be prepared," he said.

I turned to Pat and said, "Come on, Sherlock, let's go interviewing."

She headed for the sidewalk, ponytail swishing like a little red flag. I followed, inhaling her scent of fresh soap and light perfume.

THREE

The patrolman's partner was a cop I knew. Bernard had never been skinny; and since the last time I saw him, he had acquired a few more pounds. He looked like someone trying to shoplift an NBA basketball under his shirt. He stood waiting, arms crossed over his paunch, ten feet away from the vagrant. As we got nearer, he left the witness on the sidewalk and met us. He nodded at Pat, a big smile on his face.

Then to me, he said, "Not the best winter for you. First your wife, then the suspension. Everybody at the scene thought it was a clean shoot. Those guys were high on something—no telling what they would've done next."

"Thanks for coming to the funeral, and for the vote of confidence, Bernie. Last time we spoke, you were working out and on a diet. But now I'm sensing a breakup with Jenny Craig. I guess she was a bit stingy on the desserts."

He shook his head wistfully. "I never was much of a gym rat," he said, and his smile disappeared as he looked down at the ground.

Pat gave me an appalled stare.

With a sigh, I said, "Bernie, you look like you just stepped in dog shit. Sorry for the wisecrack. That was wrong of me. You're a good cop."

Bernie gave me a thumbs-up and waddled around to the driver's side of his patrol car. "No sweat, Bob. Your parody isn't always painless, but it's never mean. You're a great detective. You'll sniff it out."

Our witness sat on the curb with his back against a lamppost, some twenty feet behind the cruiser. He grabbed the post, pulled himself upright, and wove toward us. I couldn't see his face for the two ratty scarves that covered his neck and head. The rest of him was a bale of rags at least four layers deep. As he got closer, he peeled off the scarves.

He looked better with them on. A dead leaf decorated the top of his head.

"Holy saints in heaven, protect the innocents!" Pat murmured. "I've seen a prettier face on a week-old corpse."

"You're not joking," I said softly. "The top of his head looks like the hairball my cat coughed up yesterday."

The scarecrow staggered up to me. "Ya got a dollar for a cup of coffee?"

I fished some change out of my coat pocket and dropped the coins into his filthy outstretched hand.

"Thanks, man."

My eyes watered from his Eau de Barf and Piss cologne. I tried to turn back around by pivoting on one heel, but my spin had the grace of a drunken prostitute on six-inch stilettos. With one foot going west and the other east, I collided with Pat, who was trying not to breathe in. My instinctive reach to break my fall got me a fiery look. I removed my left hand from her breast.

"Sorry," I mumbled.

"We just started working together, and already I'm supporting you," Pat said.

I smiled. "That's what partners do."

Pat moved away from me and skillfully maneuvered herself upwind.

"What's your name?" she asked the witness.

He turned to face her, his pungent presence way to close to me. I quickly sidled upwind to relative safety next to Pat.

"My name's George—George of the Jungle," he said. "I stays at the rear of the container in the parking lot."

He punctuated his story with uncoordinated mouth and eye twitches as he told us what he saw last night.

"The military police was here last night. I know an army truck when I see one. Black Humvee with big mud tires. They arrested a girl and put her in the trunk of that car." He pointed to the BMW. "Den a whole bunch of blues and trucks came early this morning for the drug raid."

In his alcoholic daze, I guessed that the rambling story made perfect sense to him. "George, I don't think it was military police," I said. "And this morning wasn't a raid. You found a car with an open trunk and a dead woman in it. You signaled a passing patrol car to stop. We need you to remember everything that happened last night in your parking lot."

I beckoned to a patrolman. He looked 20 at the most. I supposed his cowboy handlebar mustache was an attempt to look older.

I pointed to George. "You'll have to bring him uptown. Have him dictate a statement to the duty sergeant in homicide."

The cowboy kid officer got a whiff of George and blinked. "In *our* car? Come on, Lieutenant, that's cruel!"

"Relax, kid," I said. "You're not being exposed to a nerve gas—just last night's drunk and a little B.O." I reached for my wallet and pulled out two twenties. "I'm leaving you in charge of the witness. Walk him the four blocks up to the YMCA, get him showered, and get his clothes washed if you can. Feed him, and don't be stingy with the coffee. Then bring him in for his statement."

With a pained look, he signaled George to follow him up the street.

"You've got a big heart, Lieutenant Bear," Pat said. "You saved the poor kid from some bang of benjy off the gyppo."

"Uh, you lost me with that one," I said. "I'll have to learn Irish slang, or maybe I can teach you French-Canadian slang. Or we both could learn signing." I made mock symbols with my fingers.

Pat looked behind me. "Speaking of signing, Dobson's waving at us."

In the short space of our interview with George, the parking lot had filled with people. Joggers and early shoppers taking a curiosity break surrounded the crime scene. Techies adjusted the parabolic antenna on the roof of a just-arrived television news truck.

"The newshounds have arrived," I said to Pat. "Beware their yapping questions. Officially, we have no comment."

We walked back toward Dobson and the BMW. Before we reached the taped perimeter, a Mutt-and-Jeff team of reporters spotted the gold badge hanging from Pat's neck and moved in on her. The short, wide one blocked her path, and the tall, skinny one thrust a microphone in her face.

Before Mutt could ask his first question, Pat brushed the microphone out of his hand in one "clumsy" sweep of her left arm and "accidentally" trampled his instep.

The wide one stepped in front of me and reached out a hand towards Pat's shoulder.

I sidestepped between them, grabbed his arm and clamped down hard on his biceps. I slowly lifted until he was on his tiptoes. He made little gasping noises as I pulled him closer to me and gave him a wide smile.

"Excuse us," I said. "We'd just like to get through." Then I swiveled him around to one side, as if opening a door.

When we had gotten a few feet away, I said to Pat, "Your guy's still hopping around on one foot."

"You didn't have to weightlift your man," she replied. "I coulda' taken care of him myself.

"That's what partners do," I said.

Pat strode ahead to the crime scene. I trailed behind, worrying that Jean's comment on my mental state may have been right. The view of the folded woman in the car trunk had gotten to me. Maybe I wasn't as tough as I imagined. Memories of Colleen fogged my thoughts. I shook my head, and my new partner's lovely backside came into focus. A hired assassin and a sexy partner—I knew that I was headed for trouble.

FOUR

The crime scene looked like another Montreal student demonstration. A crowd of people had bunched around the "Police Line Do Not Cross" polyethylene tape, all jostling to get a better view. Dobson was surrounded by a half-dozen yelling journalists begging for any scrap of information that could make it into the noon report. He fended them off as best he could. I reached into the nearest squad car, took the microphone, and, cranking the speaker system up to full blast, ordered everyone away from the crime scene.

Five minutes later, Dobson's team unrolled a black plastic sheet to serve as a barrier against the crowd of gawkers and paparazzi while they put the victim in a body bag. I helped the other officers hold up the sheet, doing what we could to protect the victim's dignity for the transfer to the morgue truck. Pat stood beside me in respectful silence as the body passed before us.

I quoted: "Here lies another box for nature, carbon ready; black to eyes down here, where death is at its job."

"What's that from?" asked Pat.

"A poem by Mark R. Slaughter—appropriate in this circumstance, I think."

After the morgue van left, Dobson called us over. He addressed me but looked only at Pat, as if I were suddenly invisible.

"We're moving the car to the lab. Nobody can clean up in a rush and not leave me some shred of evidence. I'm taking it as a personal challenge to find something the killer missed. I ran the VIN number through the system. The coupe is registered to a high-end furniture and interior design boutique called Elle Décor, on upper Saint Denis Street. Here are the coordinates."

Dobson handed me a computer printout.

I said, "Don't tell me the victim's an interior decorator. Putting out a hit because you're miffed about a paint shade sounds a bit extreme."

Pat turned to me with a frown. "Catch yourself on. Hiring professionals to murder somebody is a high-risk, expensive decision. This case is as bent as a nine-bob note. My feeling is, it's going to get complicated before the end of this."

"You may be right," I said. "You guessed that it took two to place her body, so now we're looking for a team of hit men. They sure aren't waiting around, we have to move fast. Where's your car? Let's get rolling."

"In front of the news truck," she said, pointing to a new Ford Mustang.

"Come on. The trail's growing colder by the minute."

This time I took the lead and Pat had to quick march to keep up.

FIVE

Springtime roads in Montreal were a network of fissures and potholes strung together with ribbons of asphalt. Years of neglect and shoddy workmanship from crooked contractors had taken their toll on the city's infrastructure.

Pat maneuvered her silver-gray Mustang carefully around the worst of the craters. It still smelled new. She drove cautiously, as if afraid to scratch it.

"Do you always drive like an old lady?" I said. "We're cops. We can exceed the speed limit in the line of duty, you know."

She gave me a sideways look that could have frosted the window on my side of the car.

"I just got it back from the shop, and you'll have me wreck it? Jaysus, these cratered streets feel like we're in downtown Fallujah!"

She turned east on the next street, and I shut up. As we traveled, I enjoyed the view. When you're the driver, your focus is on someone's rear bumper. You miss the living, breathing pulse of the city.

A blur in the sky caught my eye. A red-tailed hawk wheeled and dived at a neon roof sign announcing "Best smoked meat in town." White and gray feathers came loose from the impact and floated down as he flew off with a fat pigeon cock.

The law of the jungle was in full play, here in the midst of a bustling metropolis.

We traveled east and north along boulevards and narrow one-way streets. We could have saved fifteen minutes on the trip; I didn't comment and kept the peace with small talk.

"So, why switch from Fraud to Homicide?"

"Near two years of working at a computer was beyond the beyond. It gave me the hump."

"If I translate correctly, you were bored out of your mind," I said. "Not enough action?"

"Action's in my blood. My da' was a brigadier in the army; my two brothers, my uncle, all homicide detectives; two cousins in the Garda."

"You still speak with a bit of a lilt. How long have you been in Montreal?"

"At' a fact. I'm Full Oirish, but I was born here. I was two when my ma died giving birth to my younger brother. Da' moved us back to Kilkenny to be with family. I grew into the business and put in five and a half as a patrolwoman on Dublin streets. Then Da' got a bad dose of the big C and passed. Uncle Jean came for the funeral, and I decided to follow him back here. I did the fifteen weeks' refresher at the police academy in Nicolet, did the exams, passed sergeant, and found an opening in Fraud."

"And, now you're paired with me—beauty and the beast," I said.

"'At's pure bollocks; you're no beast. In fact, you're fair ride, in a primitive, rugged sort o' way."

I got a hard punch to the shoulder when I replied, "I didn't say I was the beast."

We finally made it to the store. In one smooth flow, Pat parallel-parked the car into a tight spot. I was impressed but didn't comment. We stepped out and crossed the street.

The furniture store that Dobson found listed as the registered owner of the BMW was closed. A wrought-iron grille with a stylized "E" in its center barred the entrance. Pat read a little gold sign just right of the door.

"We're a tad early. It's open ten to five, Monday to Friday."

My smartphone informed me that it was now 9:42 on Thursday morning.

"There has to be somebody in there getting ready to open," I said. "This'll get their attention."

I slid my hand between the bars and karate-chopped on the interior glass door. My knocks attracted no one.

"'At's no use," Pat said. "You hammer like a babby." She slid off one of her little gray boots and pounded the grille with the heel.

"I think you've gotten the neighborhood's attention. From inside, it must sound like a fair imitation of Big Ben."

A well endowed blonde with a yard of cleavage appeared on the other side of the glass door and scowled. She pointed to her wristwatch. I flipped open my holder and pointed to my badge. She kept her sour face as she unlocked locks and slid doors open.

I acted the gentleman and let Pat enter first.

"Morning, ma'am," she said. "This is Lieutenant Beaudry; I'm Detective O'Neil. You have a metallic red BMW M-six coupe registered to your company. Could you tell me who drives that vehicle?"

The woman stared down her nose at Pat.

"What's this about? We really don't open until ten. What's so important?"

Pat took a step toward her. "Who drives that car?"

The blonde woman's neck flushed pink as she took a step back and looked down at the floor.

"I, ah, it's Miss James's car. She's the owner."

"And is Miss James in?" I asked.

"No, no. She comes in after lunch, but she often works late after the store is closed. She didn't have an accident, did she?"

I held up my index finger to signal that it was time to shut up and listen.

"Can you tell me who's in charge when she's not here?"

"Mister Yves—he's the floor designer. Should I get him?"

Pat gave a vigorous nod, and the woman stomped off toward the rear of the store while I got a sideways under-the-lashes look from my new partner.

"I saw you didn't miss the diddies on the blonde. It's a bear or a wolf are you?"

"I'm a trained observer," I said. "You never know where you might find a clue."

A pasty-faced middle-aged man sporting a ponytail sashayed down the store's center aisle toward us. A flouncy pink hankie hung out of the breast pocket of a pinstriped suit that was too tight on him a year ago. Ignoring Pat, he looked me over and smiled.

"Yeess, Detective, can I help you?"

"Is there anywhere we can talk in private?"

He made a little Japanese-style bow, then gestured open-handed toward the rear of the store. We paraded down the long aisle, with Yves leading and me trailing.

I whispered to Pat, "I'm glad he didn't say 'walk this way.' I could have dislocated a hip bone."

Pat gave looked back at me with a small headshake and eyes raised to the sky.

"You have a nice display of furniture," I said to Ponytail. "It's a shame I didn't know about your store before I finished my renovations."

He glanced back over his shoulder. "What do you favor?" he said.

Hoping he was talking about furniture, I said, "Contemporary eclectic. I go for the simple, clean look."

"We-ell, Mr. Sophisticated Police Detective, you're in the right place. We're all about Chicago style." He hesitated for half a step and glanced back at me again. "Contemporary, minimalist, modern, but that includes organic elements. It makes for a quite unexpected but exciting experience."

I still wasn't sure he was talking about furniture. We entered an office space at the back of the store, and Yves pointed me to a visitor's chair. His pant legs rose up as he sat himself behind a neat glass desk.

"Does your car match your socks and handkerchief?" I asked.

"I don't drive. I live green," he said.

"Ignore my last comment," I said. "I understand your boss has a red BMW—"

Before I could finish my sentence, Pat touched my hand and pointed to the trophy wall behind Yves. There was a ten-by-twelve-framed picture of him with our victim. They were holding a large award plaque between them.

"In the picture behind you," Pat said to Yves, "is that Miss James?"

"Yes. That's when our store won a design award; I'll have to hang a new one to my collection, Diana just won Businesswoman of the Year."

I broke the bad news to him. Yves earned two bonus points on my interview score when, with a trembling hand, he pinched his lower lip to keep from bursting into tears.

"You'd best close the store for today," Pat said. "We need to talk to your staff, one by one. We have to get to know more about Diana in a few short hours: where she lived, who her friends were, where she went, her recent meetings and appointments—all that stuff."

"It would be helpful," I added, "if we could have her agenda, her home coordinates, and her cell-phone number."

Yves looked a little gray. He brought his hands to his temples and rubbed in little circles.

"Oh, dear, oh, dear, Diana is—was—a very private person. Her business life was totally separate from her home life. We . . . we won't be of much help, I'm afraid. Excuse me," he said in a strained voice. "I have to go to the washroom. I'll get you her schedule on my way back."

He staggered out of the office, holding on to furniture, the walls, and the doorjamb. Pat stood up and looked down at me.

"Shot dead and dumped in her car trunk. Robert, you acted like a numpty homophobic gruff bear. Do you not think, now, that you could have been more tactful with the poor fellow?"

"I've seen a world of misery," I said. "Laughing at myself and at the quirks of others keeps me moderately sane. But in retrospect, maybe I could have started with the small dent in her car and worked my way up. After my broad, manly shoulders, one of my strong points is that I am honest and straightforward. One of my weak points is that I am honest and very straightforward . . . as my new partner has so aptly pointed out."

"I'm after telling you to improve the team," she said. "That's what partners do."

Yves came back with reddened eyes, but a bit more composed. He gave us Diana's agenda and the employee list. There were a dozen employees at Elle Décor and its warehouse.

"You start with your buxom friend up front, the sales reps, and accounting," I said to Pat. "I'll take the truck drivers and warehouse guys."

* * *

We met again in Yves's office at ten after twelve. She was sitting at his desk, with a pile of documents spread out in front of her.

"I phoned Dobson and gave him Diana's name and social security number," Pat said. "I haven't found much else. Her little leopard-skin-covered business agenda is strictly business. I can't find anything at all—nothing—of a personal nature in her office stuff."

"I don't know how your interviews went," I said, "but on my side, Yves's predictions were bang-on. She kept her personal life to herself. Apart from the general consensus that she was a real bitch on wheels, nobody knows nuttin'."

"That's bogey," Pat said. "Looks like she kept her outside life secret, but everybody loved her. Even the blonde sourpuss said Diana was an angel straight from heaven."

"Strange," I said. "Unless she has an evil twin, we're getting two very different sides of her. We need to compare notes."

Pat stood up and grabbed her throat as if to strangle herself. "I've been up since ten to early. I could eat a whole cow sandwiched between two bread vans."

A very red-eyed Yves stumbled into the office as I said, "I take it that it's time for a lunch break. Yves, you were right. We pretty well wasted our time with your staff. But it had to be done."

He put a hand on my arm and handed me a large manila envelope. He looked worn out and miserable, as if he had aged ten years in the past few hours.

"I made you copies of the insurance policies on her car and house and listed the phone numbers for her accountant and personal lawyer," he whispered. "I added the address for her condo, and her spare key. I don't know what else I can do to help."

"We're truly sorry for your loss, Yves," Pat said. "Thanks for your help, and fair play to you."

"Yes," I added. "Thank you for the key. That's going to be helpful. I'll have a cute patrol officer bring it back to you."

Yves gave us a weak smile and recommended a good restaurant down the street.

SIX

A Michael Bublé tune emanated from Pat's jacket pocket just as we were about to enter the restaurant. She moved a few feet away to take the call. Even at a distance and with her back to me, I could clearly hear her informing someone that he was a "gobshite." She ended her conversation and turned off the phone.

"Your cheeks are doing a fair imitation of a stoplight," I said. "What's that all about?"

She glared at her phone and then shoved it back into her jacket pocket. "My ex-husband, Mark. He's a sleazy lawyer and a mean drunk who likes to beat on women."

I winced as if I'd been kicked in the shins. "He hit you?"

"Stay easy, big bear. He came home a couple of times smelling of perfume. I'm not stupid. I didn't have to be a copper to figure what he was up to. A few weeks later, he called to tell me he'd be working late. I took a little trip to his office that evening. Caught him boinking his secretary on his office couch."

"He must have been surprised by your impromptu visit," I said.

"He was bloody furious! We had a grand row, and he tried to clatter—ah, slap—me. I broke his nose and fractured two of his ribs. Now he's threatening to sue me."

"Remind me never to get you mad," I said.

Pat smiled, and her cheeks softened to a lighter shade of angry.

"Plus, I didn't sign his prenup. Now he refuses to give me my half of the house. Most of the furniture I bought, anyhow. The cheap bastard wouldn't give you a bean. He's changed the locks and put in a new alarm. I'm stuck in a downtown hotel for the past three weeks. He's trying to intimidate me into giving up my settlement. He harasses me with eight eejit calls a day. He follows me everywhere, but not near enough for a restraining order. He'll pop up somewhere in front of me or across the street. He's driving me loopers."

"If I can do anything, just let me know," I said. "I'm a sucker for a beautiful damsel in distress."

"Him, you could shoot holes in. I just want him out of my life."

"Remind me never, ever, to get you mad," I said, holding the door open for her.

The restaurant was Asian fusion. "This okay with you?" I asked Pat. "Leave it to Yves to suggest something new and trendy."

"I'm not difficult," she said. "I like to try new foods all the time. In Montreal, I'm spoiled."

"As a bear," I said, "I favor basic red meat and fish. I go for Italian and French cuisine, mostly."

The restaurant was decorated in Asian modern. A pair of five-foot-high gold Foo dog statues, ugly enough to scare away all demons, guarded the entrance, and red-upholstered chairs respected the Chinese traditions, but the rest was strictly contemporary decor: pale wood, light-gray walls, and a glass-topped bar. The menu indicated how spicy the dishes were with graphics of a cartoon East Asian girl. For mild, she had a smile. Spicy was the same cartoon, but her mouth was an O. Very spicy was the "O" cartoon but with beads of sweat dripping off her face. Extra spicy was the same caricature as very spicy, but her face was bright pink.

"I'll go with their version of Pad Thai with the sweaty-girl cartoon," I said. "I got enough pink for today with Yves."

"I'm looking for something under four hundred calories. A damsel has to keep trim, you know."

"Ah. Sorry if I was out of line with that damsel comment. I've never had a female partner. Jeez, that didn't come out right, either, did it? What I meant is, I generally work alone. In fact, I'm more the type that runs with scissors and doesn't play well with others."

"Not to worry," Pat said. "I've worked with men all my life, so I've developed a thick skin for off-color remarks. In fact, I now have difficulty accepting any admiring comment at face value."

I gave her my best smile, the one that, ten years earlier, used to make a girl fall right into my bed. "Well, in the words of Homer Simpson, you're as pretty as Princess Leia and as smart as Yoda. I wasn't looking forward to being saddled with a partner, but, to be honest, I'm glad to be working with you. Take it or leave it."

"I know from recent experience that you're brutally honest, so I'll accept your lopsided compliment. Speaking of honest, I was surprised that you changed from a bear to a wolf when you eyed our buxom blonde at the store."

"I guess that I'm a bear-wolf. It's better than being a werewolf."

"So not a werewolf, a werebear." Pat said with her melt titanium smile.

The waiter came to take our order, breaking the moment.

I was at ease with Pat and felt no qualms about being a bit silly. The world seemed a little brighter this morning. Maybe it was just springtime—the sad, gray winter skies were finally giving way to a more optimistic blue, bringing fresh light to everything. I was back on a case, with a cute partner. I felt alive again.

I straightened up in my chair and handed her my pocket-size spiral pad.

"Here are my interview notes. Compare them with what you found. I'll call Dobson and have him meet us at Diana's condo."

Dobson answered on the first ring.

"I was about to call you," he said. I had my cell phone in hand."

"Great minds think alike," I said. "I need you and your expertise for a house search at the victim's residence. Can you do the paperwork and meet us there? I have the key for the condo. Have a team of blues lock down the place. Nobody in or out before we get there."

I gave Dobson the address and additional information that we got from Yves: the company insurance papers on the BMW, Diana's Social Security and driver's permit number. At least, now our victim had a name, a date of birth, and some traceable history.

Dobson gave me an update from his side. "The medical examiner estimates that the victim died between two thirty and three thirty Thursday morning. The car's in the lab, and we're going over it for the second time. The killer or killers cleaned off the inside of the car with some type of oxygen bleach, but they underestimated me. I found microscopic traces of the victim's—eh, Miss James's—blood on a thread in the top seam of the driver's headrest, and traces of powder burn on the window edge. The way I read it, the killer shot her while she sat in the driver's seat. She lowered the window partway to speak to him. He rested his weapon on the window edge and shot her in the heart; then, as she bent sideways, another tap behind the ear. We extracted the slugs, both twenty-two-caliber hollow-points fired from the same weapon. From the low penetration, I'd say subsonic ammo and perhaps a silencer. Score one for the redhead. She was right on the caliber."

He rang off after confirming that he would run Diana's info through the system and that we would meet him at her condominium at two o'clock.

Our food arrived. My chopstick skills slowed the eating process and stretched my enjoyment of the meal. Pat eschewed the chopsticks altogether and ate like a pothead with the munchies. Catching my stare as she shoveled another forkful into her mouth, she slowed her frenzy enough to answer me around a mouthful of Hunan beef. "I'm chuffed. I was savage with the hunger."

I brought her up to speed with the info from my phone conversation with Dobson. She winked at me when I told her he gave her props for her keen observation at the scene.

Pat slid my notebook back across the table to me.

"With all due respect to ya, your notes are fierce Sanskrit," she said. "But from what I could glean, Miss James doted on most of the women and, with a few exceptions (including Mister Yves), was severely critical of most of the men. Herself seemed to have issues with the male gender—maybe an abusive father, or a scoundrel of a boyfriend."

"You said she was a beek—a hottie," I said. "She could have many boyfriends. Hopefully, we'll dig up something more personal at her condo.

"From my interview with one of the accounting girls, I found out that Diana was an only child and that she recently inherited a pile from her dad. A couple million quid can attract a lot of wrong sorts."

"A couple of million dollars may make a murder worthwhile, but even that doesn't make much sense. It would be easy to trace the money. There has to be something else here."

Pat glanced at her wristwatch. "We'd best stop rabbiting on and get to Diana's place. I'll get the car and meet you out front."

She dashed to the door as the waiter came up to me and handed me both bills.

SEVEN

Typical of fast changing Montreal weather, the bright spring morning had morphed into dull-gray nimbostratus clouds.

Heading to Diana James's apartment, Pat kept up with the flow of traffic.

"You've cranked up the aggression a notch, I see," I pointed out. "You really cut off that cabbie."

"I hate driving downtown," she said. "Montreal motorists' blast around like it's all one big Grand Prix racetrack. You'd swear they're a bubble off true as soon as they get wheels under 'em."

I pointed to a delivery van backing out of a lane and right into oncoming traffic. "The Gallic disregard for any type of motoring finesse runs rampant on Quebec's roads. Going from A to B in Montreal is not just a drive; it's an adventure."

As if to confirm my observation, Pat made an obscene gesture at an idiot who decided to double-park in the midst of the congested main street.

Her analysis of Quebec drivers complete, we motored on in silence, each of us in our own bubble of thought.

I had met Pat only hours ago, yet I felt as if had known her for years. I had warmed to her immediately when she called me "Lieutenant Bear." She was smart, fun to work with, and easy on the eyes. I needed to remain focused on the case; to do so; I had to disregard any feelings toward her. It was going to be difficult. At lunch, her titanium-melting smile had turned my heart to Jell-O. I promised myself to keep our relationship strictly on a professional level—a vow that I was to regret later.

On the street, I was always in control. I knew exactly how far I could push a situation. I was smart on the job, but when it came to women, I was a hopeless romantic fool. I fell in love easily and got hurt with the same ease. From my years on the job, I had pale knife scars and even a couple of bullet pockmarks. But none hurt as bad as the unseen wounds my up-and-down love life had incurred.

Maybe Jean was right: maybe, in the months following my divorce from Colleen and her subsequent death, I had been as crazy as my cat. That was another slow-healing hurt.

Colleen had craved attention. I was a high-profile detective. She delighted at the recognition people gave us in restaurants and sporting events and at seeing my face in the local papers and on the eleven o'clock news. But after a few short months of our living together, she had come to realize that my police work was more boring routine than Hollywood glamour. Colleen complained about my night and weekend shifts. In fact, a lot of her complaints flew right over my head, uncaught. She kept sending signals that something was going awry. But like a dumb felon in front of the sentencing judge, I got the message too late.

We were in a fancy French restaurant having what I thought was a romantic supper, when she pulled the pin on her news grenade, happily announcing a new job with the Canadian embassy in Ottawa. "It's a big promotion for me, and I get to go to all the embassy parties and meet diplomats from all over the world."

In shock from the concussive news, in slow motion, I lowered my glass of pinot noir from my lips back to the table.

"You're moving to Ottawa next week?"

When she answered, I knew that the relationship had run its course and that, in fact, we had already broken up.

"It's only, like, two hours away. We can see each other weekends. You're not home half the time, anyway."

Long-distance romances never work out. "Far from the eyes, far from the heart," goes the French saying. It was just a matter of time before her long, lanky body was writhing away in someone else's bed. The divorce papers had arrived two months after her departure for Ottawa.

Pat touched my hand. It startled me pleasantly back into the present.

"A penny for your thoughts," she said, removing her hand.

"With inflation, TPS, and TVQ taxes, it's probably a dollar ninety or so," I said.

We turned up the street seconds after Dobson, who grabbed the only free space in front of the condominium. Pat spied a loading zone next to a bakery and speedily parallel-parked in the empty spot, and then lowered her sun visor to show the "police vehicle" sticker.

We headed toward a patrolwoman who was guarding the entrance to a canal-side factory recently transformed into new condominiums.

Pat pointed to a billboard next to the building. "Ninety percent sold, but they still have some units left. The starting price is only four hundred fifty-nine thousand. On my sergeant's pay, methinks I'm going to have a problem finding new digs after my divorce."

"The Atwater Market area is the new trendy place to be," I said. "Close to the downtown business area, yet surrounded by parks and miles of biking trails along the old canal. After Old Montreal, this would be my second choice."

"It must be pretty here in summer," Pat said. "Let's go find out what Diana got for her half a million."

EIGHT

At the condo entrance, Dobson stood next to a slight, five-foot-three-ish patrolwoman. What she lacked in physical presence she made up for with attitude. Her eyes said, don't even think you can sweet-talk your way in here.

Dobson saluted Pat, ignored me, and reported the situation to Pat.

"The patrolman at the back of the apartment just radioed that the kitchen window is smashed in. Do we call for backup?"

Before Pat could answer, I moved in front of her and gave Dobson my "Do you really want to die today?" stare. I got a blink and a swallow in response.

"Just a reminder, Dobson. I'm in charge, and I'm all the backup you'll ever need."

Any thoughts of rebuttal ended when Officer Stern Face's shoulder radio crackled. The uniform in the rear reported what he saw.

"Ten sixty-two, I'm on the back balcony. I can see inside. It looks like the place has been tossed."

"Pat, keep everybody in front," I said. "I'll go around back and clear the apartment with the other patrolman."

I headed into the lane next to the building and walked up the back stairs to the second-floor veranda. The cop on Diana's balcony was another youngster fresh out of the academy. I couldn't believe that a skinny little kid like him could be a real cop. Maybe he was on loan from the boy-scouts. Perhaps it's another attempt to balance the ailing city budget.

Making a visor of his left hand, he peered through the smashed window into the apartment. He saw my large shadow in his peripheral vision, turned fast toward me, and blanched. I flipped my badge, and his face relaxed but didn't quite get back its normal color.

"Kid, never stand in front of a window or a door," I said. "Always peek fast around the frame. If there had been a bad guy in there, you'd be bleeding out of too many holes for the paramedics to plug."

As he had reported, there was a dinner-plate-size hole in a low bedroom window a few feet from the patio door. On the inside floor, the shards of glass were spread out on a crumpled newspaper. I turned to Boy Scout and pointed to a sticky substance around the hole in the glass pane.

"The true professional will use an electric lock pick—you can't even tell there was a break-in. Some of the less sophisticated cat burglars bring a shopping bag with corn syrup, a newspaper, and a few other food items, as if they just came out from the local market. They never have incriminating burglar tools. They paint the window with the syrup, spread the newspaper over it, and elbow-smash the glass in. There's barely any noise, and all the shards of glass fall in with the paper. No muss, no fuss."

The kid nodded.

I didn't see myself fitting through the window, so I tried the patio door. It slid open noiselessly. Again I turned to the kid.

"The second thing the burglar does, once he's in, is unlock all the exits in case he has to make a fast escape."

I pulled my weapon out of my underarm holster and, with a tilt of my head, pointed behind me.

"Stick to my back," I said. "And don't take your gun out. I don't want to get shot."

I yelled into the apartment, "Police! We're coming in!"

From the patio, we entered the dining room and the adjoining living room. The condo was built on an open loft plan: one big space for kitchen, dining area, and living room. A hallway led to the front, where I assumed the bedrooms were. Except for a little pot of wilted basil on the counter, everything in the kitchen was out of place. All the drawers were pulled out and dumped on the floor; all the cabinets were open. Someone had looked through every nook and corner.

We crossed into the living area. The furnishings were good examples of what was on sale at the Elle Décor store. The difference was that the showroom was orderly and immaculate; here, the look was early Viking pillage. Papers and books were strewn all over the floor; a reading lamp was tossed sideways on the desk chair. I sidled toward the front of the apartment, gun first, with the kid at my back. Behind the kitchen was a guest bedroom where everything seemed in its place. The next door we opened was a large master bathroom. It was evident that a good chunk of the half million was spent on this decor. Light wood panels, dark granite counter with raised white sink on one side. In the center of the space, a freestanding egg-shaped tub was positioned in front of a granite-and-wood partition. Behind the partition, a triple-wide glass-enclosed shower filled the rear wall. No crazed knife-wielding murderer was hidden behind the shower curtain. The layout was decorator magazine perfect, from the Little Mermaid soap dish to the coordinated fluffy towels that matched the color of the floor tiles.

"Wow, I really should have checked her store before doing my renovations," I said.

"The wood-and-granite blend is modern but cold," the young patrolman said. "It's a bit too masculine for a woman's place. The whole house is like a high-class hotel room. Nice, but it doesn't look lived in."

He was right; he must have earned a Boy Scout merit badges for keen urban observation and another for contemporary design. Next was the master bedroom, at the end of the hall. I slid, gun first, around the doorframe and into the room. The inspiration for the current layout was straight out of Soldier of Fortune magazine. It looked as though a mortar round had blown everything out of the dresser drawers and night tables, spreading it all over the floor and bed.

We checked out all the rooms; no one else was in the apartment.

I clicked the safety back up on my 9mm and shoved it back in its holster. The kid followed me back into the hall and to the front door. I opened it to see Pat hugging the doorframe, her Walther P99 pistol in hand and pointed up.

"See, kid, that's how to make an entrance," I said to Boy Scout.

Dobson came in behind Pat. The petite patrolwoman with the stern countenance maintained her post outside the front door. I led everyone into the living room.

"Check out each room," I said. "I need a phone bill, agenda, diary, personal documents—you know the drill."

Pat stepped next to Dobson. "We'll take the bedroom," she said.

Boy Scout walked to the desk and pointed. "There's a router and cables under the desk, but no computer."

As I pulled on a pair of police-issue pale-blue surgical gloves, I lifted my chin at him. "I'll do the search; you bag and start the evidence list."

I sifted through the mess of papers on the floor and soon struck gold with a stack of credit card statements and two recent phone bills: one for her landline and the other for her cell phone. Bending forward to shield my move, I folded one of the invoices and slipped it into my jacket pocket, then gave the others to Officer Boy Scout to bag.

"Do we log everything we take?" he said.

Unsure whether he had actually seen my surreptitious move, I took another chance. "Absolutely," I said as I palmed another unrecorded clue and hid the document behind my back.

Nowadays, police work was an endless round of documentation. Reports seemed more important than catching the criminals.

I opened my phone and dialed the number listed on Diana's cell phone invoice. A computer-generated female voice told me that the number I was trying to reach was unavailable. The system sent my call direct to voice mail, where the same dull voice announced that the mailbox was full and to try again later. So far, I was batting zero.

Pat came out of the bedroom and handed me a small stack of pictures. "These pictures—and, I'd wager herself—were in the closet," she said. "I found them in an envelope hidden in a zippered compartment of a purse. 'Mado's birthday trip to

Montreal' is scribbled on the envelope. Her wardrobe is chock-full of high-end clothes, and half the contents of the dresser drawers that are spread all over the floor were real skimpy underwear. But I don't think the vixen would have pulled your wire."

The first four-by-six was of Diana in a passionate kiss with another woman. The rest of the collection seemed to be from a party or outing: people drinking and dancing together, and only women in the pictures—no men. I added two of them to my other illicit clues and bagged the rest.

"Well, that may explain her shabby treatment of the macho men on her staff—and, perhaps, her fondness for Mr. Yves," I said.

"I'd best get back to Dobson," Pat said. "I think he's fondling the underwear in there."

* * *

After two hours of going through the apartment, we met in the dining area for a summary. Dobson handed me a small black leather folder. Inside were Diana's passport and another picture of the blonde she had locked lips with on one of the photographs.

"She's been to Cuba a couple of times, and France last September, but that's it," Dobson said. "Except for an extensive collection of, um, female-oriented sex toys, there's nothing of interest in the bedroom. I'm going to get the camera from my van and take a few pictures of the scene for the file, and that's it. Whoever tossed the place knew what he was doing and probably found what he was looking for. I'll dust, but I don't think we'll have any prints."

"Agreed," I said. "He probably wears the same brand of gloves we do."

Dobson headed outside to get his equipment and took the bagged items and list from the patrolman. I sent Boy Scout to question the neighbors about anything they might have seen or heard.

Pat picked up her purse, bending at the waist the way women do. Her skirt rose up, and I wasn't sure whether she caught my quick glance. She turned toward me. "I think we should sit and talk," she said.

Casually nodding, I said, "Then let's

NINE

As Dobson closed the entrance door headed for his van, Pat sat down on a dining room chair and pulled out her notepad.

"First of all, we know it was a professional hit. Second, somebody took her place apart. They were looking for something specific and surely found it. Her laptop is gone, along with any USB keys or backup media. No camera or other photos in the condo at all, at all. I found those hidden pictures because I have a similar purse. Your man would'na known that this brand often has a zippered compartment to hide valuables. I think the brigand who tossed the gaff was after a snapshot of something or somebody. Diana must have an indiscreet photo that involved someone rich or powerful enough to hire a team of pros. For sure, it's not a simple shag triangle."

"You may be right," I said. "They searched the apartment and found what they were looking for. Then they made sure to shut her up permanently."

Pat was frowning into her notepad. "For the life of me," she said, "I can't figure how this woman could have been involved in such a ruckus. It doesn't fit her hushed, still-in-the-closet profile."

I sat down across the dining table from Pat. "Unless we're really missing something, I don't see our Diana as a blackmailer or as somehow fitting into a gang of criminals. She didn't need the money. For somebody go to the trouble and cost of hiring professional killers, the documents or pictures, if that what it's about, must be more than embarrassing—it must be deadly incriminating."

"How did they find her?" Pat said. "And what was she doing at the Old Port parking lot that late at night, anyway?"

"There are quite a few bars and clubs around there," I said. "Closing time's three a.m., so that might fit the scenario."

"We'll have to canvass all the bars and clubs in the area and see if they recognize her in the picture you pilfered," Pat said with a grin.

"I think we may be able to shortcut the lengthy bar research," I said.

From my jacket, I took out one of the photos Pat had found in the purse's secret compartment. "The women in this picture are sitting on pink bar stools and drinking out of unusually slim glasses. There's a bartender on the other side of the counter, wearing a pink vest. I'm sure there aren't twenty bars with pink stools in Montreal. Colleen was into the bar and nightclub scene, but not me. But I do have a good friend in Vice who knows every watering hole in the city. If we show him this photo, maybe he'll identify the bar for us. Diana's girlfriend may be another piece of the puzzle. Cherchez la femme."

Pat shivered as if chilled by a sudden draft. "Her blonde girlfriend may be a piece of the puzzle, or part of the problem. Diana shoulda' had her lover's picture on the night table or somewhere. Maybe the killers have the picture. The girlfriend may be at risk herself. I've bad vibes on this."

I pulled out my phone and swiped the screen awake.

"Let's find out who we're up against," I said. "I have some bad friends—they may know if there's a team of pros on a contract in town."

I called the manager of a cheese factory that was one of the legit businesses run by the local don. I got through to his dragon of a secretary.

"Good afternoon, Marisa, Bob Beaudry for Mario . . . I know, I know, he's busy, but this is important . . . By the way, congratulations on your daughter's wedding . . . Yes, it was a hard time. Thank you for the condolences."

After more small talk, I finally got to leave a message on his voice mail: "Mario, I'm on my cell phone. I'm bidding a major job against a new team of outside contractors. Maybe your company knows my competition. I'm just looking for any advice from you or your boss. I'd really appreciate a call back."

Pat gave a snort. "And you make fun of my Oirish slang! That was a whole other level of language there, was it not?"

"In one of the fables of La Fontaine, it is said, 'Nothing is more dangerous than a friend without discretion; even a prudent enemy is preferable.' I can't just ask him on an open line if there's a new gunsel in town."

"You're on first-name terms with the local crime syndicate boss. You recite poetry rightly for the particular moment, and you quote long-dead French authors off the cuff. There seems to be more to detective bear than meets the eye."

I gave her a sly smile as Dobson came in. He and his duffel bag of tech toys trailed water drops across the floor. "The sky's black," he said, "and the possibility of rain that the weatherman hinted at this morning is now a sure bet."

I woke my phone again and called my contact on the vice squad. He answered on the second ring.

"Hi, Nico, you're on speaker. I'm with Sergeant O'Neil, my new partner. I told her you know every nightclub in town. We're looking for one with hot-pink bar stools."

"I can't think of anything offhand," Nico said. "And wazza matter you? You're still as brusque as ever. I haven't heard from you since the funeral. No 'how's the family'—niente, just 'I need info.' I hope your new partner has better social skills."

"Hi, Mr. Nico, this is Pat O'Neil. I already know that Beaudry is quite the gruff bear. I'm working on that, but he's right: we need information fast—somebody's life may be at risk."

"Patricia O'Neil—the redhead from the Fraud squad?"

"The very one," Pat said.

"Roger and I are harassing an informant late this afternoon, and then we're having supper at my uncle Carmine's new restaurant downtown. Join us. Maybe between us we can find what you need. Bring the big bear. Tell him it's my treat."

"You're still on speaker, Nico," I said. "Just give us the address and time."

After we hung up, I turned to Pat. "First off, I'm not something you can tame. Just trust me on that one. Second, you may have bitten off more than you can chew—literally. You can forget your four-hundred-calorie fair-maiden meal. Supper with Nico is always a six-course affair."

Pat took out a pen and flipped open a page of her notebook. "What's Nico's full name, and who's Roger?"

"Sergeant Nico di Lalla. He's a good cop who will probably never make lieutenant, because some members of his immediate family are on the other side of the badge. He complained about my snubbing him, but we go way back. He stayed with me the day of the funeral and bunked at my condo the next day to make sure I was okay. His partner is Roger Lamont. We call him 'Professor.' The guy has a doctorate in criminal psychology but insists on doing street work."

Pat flipped her notebook shut and put her hand on mine. "I don't want to be indiscreet, but I keep hearing about your wife's funeral. Jean told me that you took it hard. Is it okay to ask what happened?"

"Ex-wife. We'd split up months before. The divorce was scheduled for court three weeks after she died. It would have gone through uncontested. She was my favorite mistake, but we were done."

"A done mistake—'at's also a fair description of my situation. So what happened to herself?"

"After our separation, she came back to get the rest of her stuff at the condo. She drove an old-style souped-up Mini Cooper S that I rebuilt for her. It was too small to fit all her bags. So she borrowed my 'sixty-seven Pontiac GTO and disappeared with it. I left messages, but she never returned my calls. I finally reached her three weeks later. I told her it took me over two years to restore the car to its original maroon-monster status. I wanted my toy returned, period. She promised to bring it back the next day and didn't. I left her a final message, saying that if I didn't get the GTO back by the end of the week, I'd report it stolen."

"That was fair," Pat said. "So she figured on getting away with breaking your heart and stealing your car, now?"

"I'll never know what she was thinking. On the road from Ottawa to Montreal late the next night, she killed the car—and herself. They estimated she hit the overpass abutment at eighty-five miles an hour. The investigators at the crash scene couldn't figure out exactly what happened. Neither can I."

Pat squeezed my hand, and her moist eyes looked straight into mine. "Brutal hames, that. Robert, I've known you for but a day, and I already know you've a heart as wide as your shoulders. Nothing of that was your fault, so you'd best lay off the guilt. It'll just make ya daft. I don't understand why the angels took my ma and da' so young. Nor why I was stupid enough to marry Mark. And you'll never know what happened on that road. We pull up our socks and push on, partner."

I stood up, looked at her, and said, "My troubled conscience tells me I'm the one who gave her the ultimatum that put her on that road that night."

She thought for a moment before replying, "During some of the troubles in Dublin, I let my partner go down a narrow lane to check out a suspicious package. It exploded and spread him across two walls. I was in shock for days. But I realized that it was his fate and it was my fate, and fate itself didn't care a farthing. Making myself sick over it wouldn'a changed a thing."

"Look," I said, "I appreciate your concern. But be warned: you keep on holding my hand and looking at me with those soft green eyes, and I'll kiss you on the nose."

"Ah, I've suffered worse threats," she said with a grin. Then she glanced at her wristwatch.

"It's coming on half five. I can't go out to dinner dressed like this. I have to get back to my hotel and change."

I told Dobson we were leaving and to lock up and "police seal" the door when he was finished.

Pat opened the front door to pouring rain. "Jaysus, it's bucketing! 'At'll ruin my jacket."

"Not to worry, fair maiden," I said. "Mine's rainproof. Give me your car keys. I'll cross the block and pick you up here at the door."

My chivalry got me a good dousing of cold water down the collar, but when my partner got in and gave me another warm smile, I figured the drenching was worth it.

TEN

As we headed downtown, the rain slacked off. I dropped the wipers to intermittent and said, "I'll drive to my place and you can pick me up on the way back from your hotel, okay?"

"Sounds like a plan, partner," Pat said.

We were at an intersection, waiting for the light to change, our windows vibrating to the rap bass line coming from a pimped-out Acura Integra in the next lane. The low-profile wheels, air scoop, and rear deck spoiler showed the exterior changes. I could only guess at the engine modifications. The little metal-flake-red Japanese tuner rocked from side to side as if the car were alive and breathing. The driver had the bass cranked up to the pain threshold. I looked out my side window, and the backward-ball-capped young driver pointed to the front, then to the stop light—a challenge to our Shelby Mustang. The light changed to green, and I dropped the pedal. We rocketed toward the next intersection, our adversary a half car in the lead, until a taxi moved into his lane without signaling. The Acura fishtailed as the young driver tried to avoid ramming the taxi. I laughed out loud at the screech of brakes as we shot past the near accident.

"You right chancer, don't you dare bollix up my car!" Pat said, a good octave higher than her normal voice.

The kid caught up with us at the next red light and gave us the finger. I lowered my window, flashed my badge, and waved a no-no with my index finger. The kid's eyes grew, and he shrank back into his oversize jacket.

Pat leaned over the console to punch me on the shoulder. "You big oaf, my car just came back from the shop!"

"You punch good and fast but drive so slow and careful," I said. "How'd you manage an accident?"

She made a drilling motion at her temple with her right forefinger. "My demented ex-husband smashed it. He gave it to me as a makeup gift, but I went ahead with the divorce anyhow. When I left the house with my luggage, he acted the gentleman and offered to move my car out of the garage, onto our driveway. And he did, but without opening the garage door first."

"Your Mark is crazier than my cat, and that says a lot. Are you claiming damages?"

"I don't want to waste my energy on the manky blackguard. He's a crooked tax lawyer full of underhanded tricks. He'll drag me into court for years if I let him."

"Well, if he didn't treat you right, it proves he's demented," I said.

Pat turned in her seat to look at me. Her lips didn't budge, but her eyes glowed with the same warmth as her smile. My heart was Jell-O again.

* * *

When we got to my condo, the rain had stopped. My street was close to Old Montreal and served as a free-parking zone for tourists, hospitality workers, and anybody else with a quick enough eye. There was one slot left, in a puddle larger than the car. I parked the Mustang as close to the curb as I could, so Pat could get out on the sidewalk without ruining her little boots. I opened my door and waded to a dry spot close to the center of the street. The dirty water seeped into my oxfords. My feet went cold as my socks sucked up the moisture.

Pat Pat got out, skirted the puddle, and walked to where I stood in the street, on the driver's side.

"We're parked in the kiddie pool," I said. "I can pick you up and help you into the car."

I put my hands around Pat's waist to lift her up over the several feet of water that stood between us and the driver's door. From the corner of my eye, I glimpsed a tan Mercedes heading way too fast in our direction. There was no time to warn her. I lunged forward, snatching and hugging her to me, our backs to the oncoming vehicle. The speeding car passed a foot behind me. Its wide tires threw half the puddle from the road onto us. I snapped my head around to take note of the car's rapidly diminishing license plate but got only the last two digits.

I quickly let go of Pat, suddenly realizing that I was again cupping a firm, warm 34C.

"This is becoming a habit, Robert," she said.

"Sorry. It was an innocent attempt to shield you. I thought that crazy driver was going to plow into us."

She looked toward the fleeing car. "You've just met my ex-husband. And I wasn't complaining."

My drenched suit clung to me like a bar girl on a casino winner.

"I can't understand how he fecking stalks me everywhere," Pat snarled.

I pointed to a little gold crest on the side window. "There's some type of LoJack tracking device on your car," I said. "He's getting your coordinates from that."

Pat tapped the side or her head. "In trying to forget all about Mark, I also forgot he had the antitheft thingy installed when he gave me the car. The registration's in my name. I'll have 'em change the code and restrict access."

"Come up to my condo. If we dry off your jacket, we may be able to save it. Just beware of my attack cat, Crackers—he growls at strangers."

I beeped the car to lock, and we got across the street in one piece.

ELEVEN

My house is a row-style triplex with a winding exterior wrought-iron staircase. Its architecture is unique to Montreal but not so different from some of the balconied houses in New Orleans. The ground-floor unit has its entrance off the sidewalk; the second and third floors have theirs on the second-floor balcony.

I opened my door. Crackers sat at the top of the stairs, his ears back.

As we walked up, Pat said "Japers, is it a cat or a dog?"

"He thinks he's a panther, but he's a Maine coon. The males can get up to twenty-five pounds—the same as a bob cat, not as wild and fluffier.

Crackers sniffed Pat's shoes and then rubbed against her legs.

"'Crackers'—that's a strange name for a cat," she said.

"I named him that because he acts totally crazy half of time, and the other half, he gets into so much mischief that he drives me crazy."

She bent down to pet him. He stood on his hind feet and reached up to nuzzle her breast.

"His master's cat, I see."

"He's never taken to someone so quickly. You must have some Irish faerie magic that attracts and calms wild beasts."

Crackers purred loudly and continued to burrow around her bra line.

"Where's that towel you promised?"

"I'll get one," I said.

Pat stood up, and Crackers padded down the hall toward the washroom.

"Just point the way," she said. "I'm off to the loo, anyhow."

"Just follow him," I said.

The gurgle of a flushing toilet punctuated my instructions. Pat looked at me, wide-eyed. "Did your cat just flush the jacks?"

"I don't even want to talk about it," I said. "Somehow, he's learned to activate the lever on the tank. He likes to watch the water go around in the bowl. Eight or nine times in a row, at two in the morning, can get a bit annoying."

As Pat walked down the hall, my phone thrummed its tune. The display screen showed that Captain O'Neil was my caller.

I answered. "Beaudry."

"Robert, I have Dobson's report on my desk. I'm reading the statement from your witness, George Banks. He said that two men, one clean-shaven and bald, the other with long hair and a full beard, drove up in a black Hummer and nudged the victim's car. The bald guy got out and showed her a badge. When she opened her window, George ducked back behind the container. He was afraid they were military police who wanted to put him in the brig for going AWOL. He thought they were questioning her about his whereabouts. He's a vet from the first Gulf War who came back a tad bent."

"He looked a bit off when we questioned him," I said. "Did you get anything we can use from his story?"

"He said he didn't hear any shots," Jean said. "But he did hear one man ask the other if they were going back to the mountain place or were they staying in town. George said the man said all this in Arabic. And yes, Mr. Banks does speak quite a bit of Arabic. In fact, he speaks too much, period. He was blabbing his story to a reporter before he even got out of the building."

"Arab hit men," I said. "This is getting weirder by the minute." I told Jean what we had found at Diana's apartment.

Pat walked back as I ended the call. "Your cat's destroyed your electric toothbrush and broke a little cuppy thing next to the sink."

"Figures. He always hated the sound of that toothbrush."

I gave Pat the gist of her uncle's phone call as she stepped toward the stairwell.

"We seem to have the basics of what happened, "I said. "Hopefully, we find the nightclub, and then the girlfriend can tell us more."

"I'd best be going or we'll be late for our meeting with your friend Nico," Pat said. "I'll ring you when I leave my hotel."

She went down the stairs without a backward glance. At the sound of the closing front door, the apartment suddenly felt very empty.

TWELVE

Pat's Mustang made the unmistakable burble-burble sound of a big V-8 as we cruised down the street in low gear. My partner was back in the driver's seat, and I was navigating, though not very well. We went around the block three times, and I still couldn't find the address. Pat pointed to a 1920s three-story baroque building.

"That should be it," she said. "No number on the building, so you have to extrapolate it from the next one up and the next one down."

"Okay, Sherlock. In my defense, it doesn't look like a restaurant. It looks like a bank. Stone pillars and gargoyles on an aged copper roof."

We parked close and walked up to the massive oak door. A discreet brass plaque next to it announced, "Carmine's fine Italian cuisine."

"Looks like a private club," Pat said.

"Nico always goes to high-end joints," I explained. "Vice cops can probably justify big expense accounts."

We stepped inside. The place was redundant with marble, hand-rubbed wood, and polished brass. We headed into the dining room, where a silver-haired headwaiter stepped out from behind a frosted-glass partition to intercept us.

"Bonjour, monsieur, madame," he said with a stiff smile.

"We're supposed to meet Mr. Di Lalla," I said. "Do you have a reservation in his name?"

"Ah, yes! Monsieur Nico—the private salon."

He flashed us a more genuine smile, straightened his little bow tie, and stepped ahead of us. "Please follow me," he purred.

We went around the frosted-glass partition. On our right side, a round polished stainless steel door hung open on its channeled frame. The opening was wide enough to drive a midsize car through. As we passed, I saw hundreds of wine bottles safely stored behind a climate-controlled glass partition, their foil-capped heads all tilted slightly downward, as if bowing politely to the outside world of wealthy patrons who would buy them.

I nudged Pat and nodded to the right. "So it was a bank," I said. "They used the old vault for the wine cellar. They have quite a collection."

"We'd best be dog wide on our manners at this eating house," said Pat.

"We may have to leave your car as a deposit," I replied.

The silver-haired maître d' led us past a few doors. The smell of cigar smoke and marinara sauce wafted through one of the open doors. Heavy red velvet drapes framed the windows, and the walls were wallpaper reproductions of Venice's Grand Canal, with gondoliers at the perch.

Our tuxedoed guide stopped at the third door, knocked politely, and opened it without waiting for a reply. This room was even more ornate than the one we had just passed. The frescoed ceiling pictured little cherubs dangling from gold-leaf trellises that surrounded a Roman scene of Bacchus having a wild party. The decor had the mark of a manic Sicilian decorator with an unlimited budget.

Pat walked in, and Nico sprang to his feet as if he'd sat on a tack. He addressed both of us while looking only at Pat.

"Good evening. A pleasure to meet you, Patricia," he said.

Pat had untied her ponytail so that her red hair hung in soft curls to her shoulders. She took off her raincoat to reveal a slinky black dress. It fit her like a cotton T-shirt coming out of a summer rain shower.

Nico beat me to the only word that came to my mind. He stared a moment, then lowered his gaze to her feet. "Wow. Great . . . um, shoes. Sit, sit!"

He made short, sweeping motions indicating the empty chair next to him. Pat gave me a wink as she sat down.

Nico was handsome—a roguish face and short jet-black hair. He was always clean-shaven but with a blue shadow of a beard, whatever the hour of the day. His slim frame was always draped in flashy clothes. He looked like a full-page shot out of GQ. His potbellied partner, "Professor" Roger Lamont, looked his opposite. He wore his usual frumpy gray suit and no-longer-quite-white shirt without a tie. Roger was ordinary: light brown comb-over and a soft face with no outstanding traits. He would have made a perfect spy. He looked like Everyman and Nobody. He stayed seated and gave me a fast three-finger Boy Scout salute.

"This is quite the place Uncle Carmine has," I said.

But no one was listening. I was invisible again. Watching Nico drool over Pat, my shoulder muscles suddenly tightened, I had to admit to myself that perhaps I was a teensy bit jealous. I took a deep breath, went across from Nico and Pat, and slouched into the chair beside Roger.

Nico said to the maître d', "Pierre, start our lovely guest here with your marvelous caprese con mozzarella di bufala."

A minute later, two waiters came into the room, rolling service trays heaped with enough food to sate a small village. The silver-haired maître d' followed with four bottles of wine, two in each hand. Nico jumped up and took Pat's plate.

"Allow me to serve you, bella rossa," he said.

With enthusiasm, he scooped a little of this, a lot of that, onto the plate.

"Ah, bene. First we eat; then we talk. Patricia, this food is so good, you'll have to go to confession after tasting it."

Pat looked at her filled plate. "I'm a bit behind on my church going these days Nico, but this does look yummy."

Pat ate like a starved lioness. True to her Irish heritage, she kept up her end of the wine quaffing. As the dessert tray rolled in, my phone played its tune. "Unknown" showed on the screen.

"Beaudry speaking," I answered.

A gruff voice said, "Lieutenant Beaudry, this is Antonio, a friend of Mario's family. Are you sure your victim was a professional hit?"

"Yes. Double tap with a silenced twenty-two—heart and head," I said.

"We need to meet," Antonio said. "Breakfast, tomorrow. Eight thirty at the Trattoria d'Oro, one street up from your house." He hung up.

A meeting one street up from my house, Antonio said. I was pleased that my mob connections were so quick to help me, but a little disturbed that they knew my home address.

I pulled out Diana's photograph of the partying girls, with the pink-vested barman in the background. I stretched across the table and handed it to Nico.

"Any idea where this could be?"

Nico kept his eyes on Pat and barely glanced at the picture. "Roger has an incredible photographic memory," he said, handing the picture over to his partner.

Roger rubbed his forehead with his fingertips as he studied the photo. "From the bar stools and general layout, it has to be Pink's," he said. "It's the new trendy gay bar in town. They opened about a year ago."

"We thank you, Professor, and thank you, Nico, for the feast," I said. "We hate to eat and run, but we're off to the gay village."

I spent a few seconds on my smartphone and found the location for the nightclub.

"I ate too much," I said to Pat. "You'll have to roll me to the car."

"That Ripasso we were drinking was excellent," she said. "But I'm a wee bit fluthered. Methinks you'd best do the motoring."

We left the restaurant, and Pat linked arms with me. The spring day turned to a brisk evening, but, warmed by the wine and good food and present company, I didn't feel the chill. I floated across the cool asphalt, buoyed by my partner's closeness.

THIRTEEN

Our headlights bounced Daliesque patterns off water-filled potholes as Pat's faithful Mustang steed carried us to Pink's. As we approached the nightclub, a truck pulled out from a delivery zone four car lengths from the entrance. I slid the Mustang into the vacated slot, did the police-card-on-the-visor thing, and we headed for the bar.

"We're out for supper and then a nightclub," Pat said. "This is like a date, Robert, even if it's a bean-flicker pub.

"No date," I said. "This is strictly police business. The rule is, no fraternizing in the same department." I instantly regretted saying it.

She pulled me toward the club entrance. "Okay, no date."

I looked down at her. Her freckled face had a pink tinge, and her green eyes were a bit glazed. She looked about half sloshed. I didn't comment.

Walking into the club gave me the feeling that we had jumped through a time warp to the year 2240. The decor was Day-Glo plastic, industrial metalwork, and aluminum scaffolding. I supposed wood and leather would be extinct by the twenty-third century.

My eyes adjusted to the gloom. The lighting was set at two notches below dim. On the central dance floor, a hundred or so people of both sexes—or maybe more—gyrated to cacophonous racket that the DJ was pumping out of the car-size speakers that surrounded her. The dancers moved in stop-motion, illuminated briefly by pulsing laser beams and rotating colored lights emanating from somewhere up in the pitch-black ceiling. The central dance floor was flanked by three better-lit smaller rooms, each with a U-shaped central bar and the same spindly pink stools as in Diana's pictures.

I nudged Pat and pointed. The barman from Diana's photo was serving in one of the side halls. We headed across the dance floor, Pat in the lead, weaving and bobbing through the stroboscopic wall of dancers. Both men and women smiled appreciatively at her as she passed. My tai chi footwork helped me tread between the dancers as I followed in her wake without stepping on toes or crashing into anyone. In the alcove part of the bar, the brightness was set to romantically dim. Now I could fully appreciate my view of Pat's splendid backside as she walked ahead of me.

The barman was wearing a pink-sequined sleeveless jacket over a black silk shirt. Though I couldn't see below the bar, I presumed he was wearing matching black pants, but then again, it could just as easily be a loincloth, or leather chaps and nothing more. He was wiping a wineglass with precise, delicate motions. I signaled him over. As he pranced toward us, I asked Pat if she wanted a drink.

"Just a cola," she said.

It seemed a wise choice. My mouth was dry, and I needed something to dilute the tidal wave of wine we'd had with dinner.

The barman raised his neatly trimmed eyebrows and gave me a quizzical smile.

"A diet cola for the lady, and two for me," I said.

He flicked his hand out over the bar to place a little pink-and-white cardboard coaster in front of me. I reached out and put my hand on his. He jerked back instinctively, but my baseball mitt of a hand had his delicate palm clamped to the bar top. With my free hand, I undid my jacket button and gave him a peek at the badge on my belt and the gun under my arm.

"Just a quick question, please," I said, releasing his hand.

His Adam's apple bobbed twice as he swallowed and nodded yes.

From my jacket, I pulled out the photo of Diana kissing the blonde girl. "I need names to go with the picture," I said. Have you seen these women?"

He made a little pout and shrugged his shoulders. I looked at him sideways, gave him a crooked smile and a head shake. I handed him the picture of Diana at the bar with him in the background.

"Try a little harder to remember," I said.

His Adam's apple bobbed again, and he leaned over and dropped the second picture onto the bar, over the photo of smooching Diana. His hand darted back to his side.

"They're not regulars," he said. "I've seen them around a couple of times in the past few months. I don't know their names."

My smile changed to a scowl as he left to get our drinks. He came back and put down glasses filled with chipped ice and garnished with a slice of lime hanging on the rim. Then he dipped below the bar and plunked down two unopened cans of Coke next to my glass. Pat's, he opened and poured with a smile.

"They sometimes hang out with Cathy," he said to Pat.

He pointed to a wispy blonde in a pageboy do, five stools down the bar. Pat picked up the pictures from the bar top and made her way over to her while I poured my first Coke.

Pat squeezed in and put her arm around Wispy's shoulders. She looked up from her drink and took in the dazzling stranger, I'm sure the rest of the room went invisible. Barely two minutes later, the two of them were huddled over the pictures spread on the bar and chatting away like teenaged classmates.

I heard a growl from somewhere behind me and turned to see a large-framed woman with a power lifter's build bearing down on Pat and the wispy blonde. She wore jeans and a bulging tank top and had short, curly hair dyed in streaks of black and light blue. The look in her eye said, get away from my girl, run while you still can!

She was still ten feet away when Wispy jumped off her bar stool, arm outstretched, palm out. "No, honey!" she yelled at the oncoming Amazon.

"Honey" ignored the plea and cocked an arm the size of mine as she bore down on the offending redhead. I was off my stool and moving, but before I could close the distance, Pat slid off her aluminum bar stool, swung the base up, and caught the big woman across the diaphragm. She grunted and bent over gasping, the wind knocked out of her. Several girls at the bar clapped, and a couple cheered. It seemed Pat had just bested the local bully.

When I reached them, the big woman was dazed but still standing, and Pat held the stool high above her head, swinging it slowly a couple of inches side to side, like a cobra ready to strike.

"Whoa—time out," I said.

Pat slammed the stool upright on the floor in front of the big girl and, in a voice that would have made a boot-camp sergeant major proud, said, "Sit."

The black-and-blue-haired woman plunked herself down onto the stool. The wispy blonde, tears welling from her eyes, rushed over to hug her wobbly girlfriend.

Within minutes, a throng of admirers had surrounded Pat. Occasionally, I would glimpse her red curls like the bull's-eye in the circle of women. And by the time Pat ordered a scotch neat for her blue highlighted opponent and a Manhattan for Cathy, the wispy blonde, I was invisible once again.

The gaggle of girls continued their evening with pink or orange test-tube shooters, so I voted myself designated driver and stayed with soft drinks.

Two and a half hours later, Pat was kissy-kissing good-bye with Cathy and her rough-edged girlfriend, and we had the name and phone number of the limo service that Diana and Monique, the blonde in the photo, usually called when leaving the club.

Pat snuggled up to me and said, "Lesh go. Our work ish done here."

FOURTEEN

In the car, as I helped Pat buckle her seat belt, she leaned into me and said, "I've had a grand time tonight. I'm fair flah'ed out. "You're nicesh."

She straightened up in her seat as tears streamed from her eyes.

"Are you okay?" I said. "What's wrong?"

"Issh me Da', divorsh, and stuff. It juss caught up to me. Not to worry. We Oirish do sadness well." She ended her sentence with a delicate snore.

The little tube-y drinks she was pounding down with all the girls must have packed a muscular punch for their size. I felt responsible for my partner. I couldn't just dump her off at her hotel—I'd have to bring her back to my apartment.

The traffic at three a.m. was the reverse of three p.m.: few people on the road, no construction work or traffic jams. In fifteen minutes, I pulled into a miraculous empty spot in front of my door. I shook Pat's shoulder gently but got no response.

"Wakey-wakey," I said. "I think you'd best sleep it off at my place."

Her snores were more robust than delicate now, sounding a little way this side of a chainsaw. She was sleeping like a two-year-old, playing strong in dreamland but limp as a marionette in this world. I managed to sleepwalk her out of the car and up the first flight of stairs. At my front door, her knees went as liquid as the high-test drinks she had imbibed.

"I'm going to have to carry you upstairs," I said. "You've gone all wobbly."

"I can't feel me feet. A'm gee-eyed. You're carrying me 'cross the threshold. Married now, are we?"

"I wish," I said. "Tuck your arm in; I'll have to go sideways."

"You're a nice fella," Pat said as the tears started rolling down her cheeks again.

Once upstairs, Pat mumbled an Irish folk song and staggered zombie fashion into the bedroom. I managed to get her raincoat off. Although tempted to continue the unwrapping, I left her dress on, put her in my bed, and covered her up. She was back on delicate cycle with the snores. I took a pillow off my king-size, grabbed a spare blanket, and headed for the living-room couch.

An hour or so later, the cry of a wildcat broke the silence of the night. I remembered that I had let Crackers out before leaving for supper.

I padded to the kitchen wearing only my boxers. Crackers dangled spread-eagled by his claws in the center of the patio door. He was plastered against the screen. Here and there, little tufts of his white belly fur poked through to my side of the mesh. Backing down from his perch, he stood in front of the door. I slid it open.

"Don't just sit there in a sulk," I said. "Get in here."

Crackers took one look at his empty bowl and let out another complaining yowl.

"You're a total nutcase. You need your breakfast at the crack of dawn. I can't stand the smell of your fishy food this early in the morning."

As I went to the cupboard, I heard Pat's steps from behind me.

"I heard a frightful cry," she said. "I thought Crackers was in agony."

I closed the pantry door. With the economy-size cat food bag in my hand, I turned to face her.

"Saints in heaven!" she said. "You really do look all muscled up like that Terminator guy, Arnold What's-his-name."

I did a Jack Benny shrug. Pat was wearing one of my favorite cotton twill sport shirts. It looked like a blue plaid tent on her. Still, she looked good in it. She took the bag from my hand, bent her knees, and filled Crackers's food bowl.

She straightened up and caught me ogling. "Heaven help me!" she said. "I'd best get back to bed before I put any silly ideas into your head."

We both went back to our beds. I didn't have any silly ideas in my head. They were farther south.

FIFTEEN

The couch was a half size narrower than I. After a fitful night of tossing and turning, I got up and sneaked into my bedroom to grab a few clothes.

Pat was still sawing logs. She lay on her back with one gorgeous leg dangling over the side of the bed but had the blankets pulled up to her nose. Crowding the pillow beside her, Crackers looked like a cartoon version of a dead cat. He, too, was on his back, with one front paw bent and the other three splayed in the air. All that was missing were the little X's over his eyes.

Breakfast could wait till my meeting with Antonio, my contact from the local crime syndicate. But Pat would be starving when she woke up. On vacation time for the past few months, I was accustomed to shopping every day, European style. My refrigerator inventory this morning was lumpy milk and fermenting orange juice. I left Pat a note and headed for the local pastry shop.

I walked out into a bright, clear morning. The sidewalks were rain-washed clean, the air smelled of wet earth, and little green buds were popping out on bush and branch. People on their way to work smiled for no good reason. Strange what spring sunshine can do!

At the street corner, I told the faded yellow self-serve newspaper box that I didn't have change and to put it on my tab, then absconded with the early edition.

The French pastry shop on the corner was doing a brisk business. Patrons were in line, ordering coffee in various blends with the obligatory morning croissant, muffin, or other artery-clogging tartlet. I grabbed a shopping basket near the door and filled it with one or two of everything.

While waiting at the checkout line, I browsed my newspaper. A familiar face stared back at me from page two. The heading read, "Homeless man questioned in brutal murder." The column scrolled around a picture of George, after his shower. I learned that he had earned a few medals for valor during his stint in the army. The article detailed the discovery of the body but touched only superficially on the facts of the case. It went on to berate the Montreal police for the lack of security in parking lots. The reporter blatantly omitted any mention of Montreal's second-lowest crime rate in the country, or that the murder statistics were the lowest in the past forty years. Favorable statistics and good news don't sell newspapers.

The store owner commented on the lovely weather. I agreed, paid my bill, and headed back to the condo.

SIXTEEN

Pat, still in her fetching blue plaid tent, had set up my laptop on the breakfast table and was clicking away.

"You look like a hacker on a high," I said.

"I am. You have your talents; I have mine. You were a bit of a dosser using 'Crackers' as your password. By the way, I upgraded the software on your router and changed your browser. What you were using was shabby."

"How's your head this morning?" I said. "You were pretty well schnockered last night."

"Oh, I wasn't twisted in the slightest—drank just enough to thin the blood."

"Oh, yeah? I carried you up the stairs."

"That's what partners do," she said with a smirk.

"I have to meet a contact. If you're hungry, I'll make you something before I leave."

"You're a psychic—I'm bloody famished."

I turned on a couple of burners, rummaged in my bag of victuals, and started banging pots. When I was done, I draped a dish towel over my left arm in imitation of a waiter and arranged several plates in front of her.

"Ze chef special today is our country breakfast," I said. "Le scrambled eggs with mushrooms and chopped chives, crisp bacon, and le multigrain toast, lightly buttered."

Pat laughed as heartily as she ate.

"Are you always this silly in the morning? On the job, you always try and act so serious—a real hardchaw."

"At home is at home. I leave the job on the street."

"'At's wise, else you'd wind up off your nut for sure," Pat said.

"The only unbalanced psyche around here walks on four feet," I said.

Crackers sauntered in and rubbed against Pat's leg.

"Speak of the wild Divil, and he appea—Jaysus, Mary, and Joseph!" she yelped.

While she spoke, Crackers had bounded up onto the table, stolen the last strip of bacon off her plate, and run off with it toward the bedroom.

I pointed to the fluffy black tail disappearing around the corner. "I rest my case, Your Honor."

Pat snickered. "Both of you look a bit wild-animal-y this morning. The cat's fur is every which way, your hair is tousled, and your face is fuzzy."

"I've got eighteen minutes to shave and shower," I said. "There's fresh coffee in the pot. Need anything else before I leave?"

"Just the pile of stuff you lifted from Diana's place: her phone and credit card bills. I've hit a wall with the limo company. They won't give me info on their clients without a court order. But last night, Cathy gave me the driver's name. I'm tracking him down now. I have hits on Facebook and LinkedIn, and I haven't gone Dogpile, metasearch, or Turbo-ten yet."

"This computer-nerd lingo is more complicated than your Irish slang," I said.

I got the stack of illicit evidence from my jacket, kept the picture of Diana and Monique, and gave the rest to Pat. Before leaving, I asked her again if she needed anything.

"Go do your meeting," she said. "I'll work here some and then go to my hotel to get changed. Call me later; I'll pick you up."

It felt strangely nice to leave the apartment and not leave it empty.

SEVENTEEN

I made it to Antonio's suggested breakfast place with a minute to spare and commandeered a window table where I could sit and admire the pretty girls of Montreal unhampered by long winter coats. The day was bright, and life was good.

A stooped, gray-haired waiter came to my table with menus in hand.

"I think you'd be better seated at another table, sir," he said. "Please follow me."

"I'm waiting for someone," I said. "I'm fine here."

"Your someone, has asked me to bring you to your table."

I followed him past the kitchen, into a small office. A café table and two chairs had been set up against the desk. I sat down in one of the chairs. The waiter straightened up and removed first his apron, then his gray hair. The transformation surprised me. In an instant, the man was rejuvenated by thirty years. He was a muscular five feet six. There were no angles to him; everything was round. His head, topped with an even fuzz of dark hair, looked as if he had shaved it just a few days ago. If not for those coal-black eyes, he would have had an almost kindly face. His physique reminded me of a fire hydrant.

He sat across from me, his back to the desk.

"I'm Antonio," he said, and stuck out his hand.

His handshake grip confirmed my fire hydrant impression.

"You always walk around disguised, or was that just a private show for me?" I said.

"I was told you're a straight shooter, in all meanings of the term, and that I could trust you. But I stay alive by being careful. In any case," he said, "you have your own disguise. Black leather jacket, jeans, and cowboy boots doesn't look like the average cop to me."

"You're careful and prepared," I said. "When you took off your apron, there was a lump in your left pocket—a compact three-eighty, I'd guess. And when you sat down, your shirt hiked up an inch in the shoulders. You're wearing Kevlar."

"Silent Partner T-shirt, Level Two. Never leave home without it. The weapon is a Kel-Tec P-thirty-two—light, accurate, and less noise than a three-eighty."

I asked him, "So when did you make the change from fists to firearms?"

"You picked up on the scar tissue in my eyebrows. Very observant, Beaudry," he said. "You're a pro; I'm a pro. So what do you say we open a window and let the testosterone fumes out and get to business."

"Okay, Antonio, business it is. You can call me Robert, but only if I get a decent breakfast."

He reached to the desk behind him, grabbed the phone, and pressed one of the buttons without looking. "Jackie, bring two truck driver specials to the office," he said, and hung up.

"My instructions are to help you if I can," he said. "The boss doesn't like to be surprised by newscasts of gun action in town. He feels disrespected if it was done without his knowledge or permission. He'd like to find the shooters as much as you do. What do you have so far?"

"Like I told you over the phone, the victim was done by a pro. It looks like they boxed her car in. The killer got out and showed her a badge. She lowered her window. He rested the silencer on the edge of the partially opened glass, and, pop—a twenty-two an inch above the heart. When she slumped forward, another shot behind the ear. End of story."

"You said 'they.'"

"A vagrant was hiding behind a Dumpster. He caught part of it. He was drunk as a skunk—smelled like one too—when I questioned him the next morning. He said two military police in a black Hummer, one bald and clean-shaven, one with a full beard and long hair. Both of them medium height, and get this: he said they spoke Arabic to each other."

Antonio scratched the top of his fuzzy head. "Not military, for sure. Not cops, not any of our team. And I checked around: not the motorcycle crowd or local gangbangers. I'm not sure I can help you out. Why would somebody need an outside pro for such an easy hit? Is the woman important?"

"From what we have so far, she was well off financially," I said. "A successful local store owner, she made Businesswoman of the Year. It's going to be a mess in the newspapers. The only other thing we found out is that she was in a relationship with a tall, hot-looking blonde."

"What about the girlfriend?" Antonio said. "Cherchez la femme."

"That's exactly what I told my partner: 'find the woman.' We're on her trail now."

I pulled out the picture of Diana and her girlfriend from my jacket pocket and handed it to Antonio. "This is the victim, Diana James, and her girlfriend, Monique."

He took the photo as my phone rang. The screen showed my home phone. I took the call.

Pat spoke in one long sentence, as if she was in a rush. "Robert, I've got the phone for the limo driver, but he's not answering. I used Diana's cell phone bills to find who she called often. Monique should, for sure, be one of them, but there was no Monique at all, at all. I do have tons of calls to a number registered to

Starlight Modeling. I hacked the cell-phone company records, and the address they send the invoices to for the Starlight account is in the Bahamas. I hit another brick wall. I'm leaving for my hotel. Is the key you left on the counter to lock up?"

"Yes," I said. "You can keep it, just in case Crackers needs a cat sitter. Just saying."

"I get a key now, do I? That's dead-on. I'll c—"

Antonio had grabbed the phone out of my hand. It looked like a magic trick: in a blink, the phone disappeared from my hand and appeared in his.

"He'll call you back," he said to Pat. He hung up the phone and slid it back across the table to me.

"Beaudry, the brown stuff just hit the fan," he said. "The blonde works for my boss."

"Back up a notch, Antonio," I said. "Monique works for the mob?"

The office door opened, and a waitress came in with heaping plates.

"Put everything on the table and get lost," Antonio said to the waitress.

She plunked our plates down and slammed the door as she huffed out. We both attacked our mountainous breakfasts as Antonio continued.

"It took me a minute to recognize the broad," he said. "Name's Monique Menard. She runs an exclusive high-end call-girl operation. My boss is not going to like this complication one bit."

"Are you serious? Diana's girlfriend runs a cathouse for the mob?" I said.

"Robert, we're not overly fond of the "M" word. And get the wax out of your ears. Yes, she runs a very exclusive, very profitable in-and-out call-girl service named Starlight Modeling. It caters to rich and influential people with kinky desires. Her being gay makes sure there are no problems with the johns. She's not interested, and she's the only one they can't buy. Keeps it strictly business."

"Crap. My partner was right: this case is bent. She's found Starlight Modeling but not the address. The mail goes to a drop in the Bahamas. Antonio, I'm going to need a local address for Monique. We have to talk to her. If she's not involved, she may be at risk herself."

"I have to step out for a minute to make a call," he said. "I have to talk to the boss before I can give you Monique. As for her safety, we have a bodyguard on-site."

He stepped out, and I speed-dialed Pat's phone.

"Robert, you mutt! Who hung up on me?"

"Sorry for that. I'll tell you the story later. Monique's involved in a mob business; I'm trying to get her address from my contact."

"Never mind," she said. "The limo driver called me back. Monique lives in a big mansion in upper Westmount. I have the address."

"Well done, partner!" I said. "I'll ring you when I'm back at my place. We'd better call on Monique before the mob shuts her down or the hit men get her."

Pat hung up as Antonio came in.

"My instructions are to help you any way I can, provided you promise to keep our operation out of your reports and out of the news."

"Well, you know, my reports are sloppy at best," I said. "I can omit a few details here and there, but I won't do anything patently illegal. As for the press, I haven't forgotten their lopsided coverage of the hostage situation I was in charge of last September." I raised the tall finger in a general salute to reporters everywhere.

"The boss seems to trust you," Antonio said. "I'll let you meet Menard. I'll give you her coordinates."

"Never mind," I said. "My partner, Patricia, is a computer hacker disguised as a cop. We have the address in Westmount."

"I'm impressed. The Starlight operation is shielded by several blind companies, including the one in the Bahamas. She's good if she managed the link between Menard and Starlight and got the address. Maybe we can make her a better offer working our side of the street."

"My partner is off limits," I said. "You just lost all your brownie points with that last suggestion."

Antonio slid a business card across to me. All it had printed on it was a phone number.

"To reach me, you can call this number any time of day. Nobody else but you."

"I have to interview Monique as fast as I can," I said. "She may be the key to all this. I'd better get my butt in gear."

"Never run when you can walk, Beaudry," Antonio said. "Speed kills. And then it's too late to say 'I should have come up with a better plan.' Always, always, have a plan. Relax, finish your French toast. We may both need all our energy on this."

Antonio was right. I survived by being fast and strong, but I would often create a mess in the process. He survived in his deadly profession by being careful and thinking things out before jumping into the fray. I relaxed and enjoyed my meal.

EIGHTEEN

Back at my condo, I phoned Pat. I got the generic female-voice message telling me that the customer is unavailable and to leave a message.

"I'm home. Pick me up anytime you're ready," I said to her voice mail.

I fed Crackers his second breakfast, cleaned up his shredded toilet-paper mess in the living room, repotted a plant that apparently had offended him, and washed the morning dishes—all before Pat called me back.

"Robert, I'm on my way."

"Good," I said. "I was getting impatient. We need to get to Monique's place as fast as we can."

"George is—"

"Yes, I know. I saw the morning papers. What a blabbermouth. I'll bet he managed to bum quite a few drinks from the reporters for that interview."

"Wheesht a minute, you big oaf of a bear—listen to me, now. George Banks, our witness, is dead."

"George the Hairball is dead? What the hell happened?"

"The poor sod was killed in a hit-and-run early this morning. From the witnesses' statements, it was deliberate. It looks like our killers are still in town and tying up loose ends. A big black truck ran him down—crossed the curb and swerved into him. He got dragged fifty feet and wound up squished against a lamppost. I've just left the scene. It wasn't pretty. This case is wrecking me nerves, Robert."

"Take it easy, partner. Homicide cases are generally messier than fraud. Our work starts with a dead body; then we go on the hunt for the murderer. Once the dice have been thrown and it comes up 'life sentence,' all bets are off. The killer has nothing to lose—one, two, or three murders are all the same price."

"Well, they better pay a price for this one," Pat said. "George was just a poor lost soul. It was cruel to kill him that way."

"Look," I told her, "you told me not to wallow in a guilt trip or I'd go off my nut. You were right. The same principle applies to our entire job. You have to stand back from the victims and look at incidents from a hundred feet above. Otherwise, as you put it, you go loopers. Come pick me up. I'll be waiting outside. When you get here, I'll give you a kiss on the nose if you need one," I said.

"Thanks for the support speech, Big Bear. I'll take a rain check on the nose kiss. I may need it later. I still have those bad vibes."

She hung up, and I mentally kicked myself for the kiss-on-the-nose comment. Around Pat, I acted like a moonstruck teenager. I had never been this silly. I vowed to stop thinking with my heart and use my brain instead.

Pat had been right when she said the case would be bent and complicated. Like a flu epidemic, our investigation was moving through all social classes: a high-end interior designer, a delusional paranoid homeless alcoholic, and a madam. Killing George by running him over in broad daylight didn't have the signature of the professional who shot Diana. The number of bad guys may have grown beyond the two we initially figured on. The idea that a simple photograph was the cause of Diana's murder now looked a bit lame.

Maybe Monique would give us another piece of the puzzle.

NINETEEN

While waiting in front of my house, I spent ten minutes admiring a house wren as it flitted back and forth to the stunted maple across the street. Intent on renovating her nest, she had just flown back with six inches of frayed clothesline when Pat drove up.

Diana's girlfriend lived in an older part of Montreal, in a district that sloped down from the mountain. Westmount is the equivalent of Nob Hill in San Francisco, Spring Valley in Washington, or the Hamptons in New York. Walled estates and small castles are the neighborhood norm. Monique Menard's address was on a one-way boulevard lined with forty-foot oaks. The squirrel population was having a let's-celebrate-spring street party. Pat let out a yelp, narrowly missing one of the fuzzy-tailed rodents as it darted from the sidewalk to the center of the road, changed its mind, and sped back to its tree in little irregular zigzag jumps.

I said, "I guess that's why erratic behavior is said to be 'squirrelly.' And speaking of erratic, our wild-haired and fragrant George must have left something out of his statement. He probably saw something he didn't tell us. He certainly had information they didn't want known."

"I figured the same," Pat said. "I asked Dobson to go though George's stuff behind the container and to sift the contents of the garbage bin. He wasn't too happy."

"We have the guns; he has the tech toys," I said. "Everybody has a job to do. And speaking of guns, you carry yours in your purse. You're not on the fraud squad anymore; you're in Homicide. Clip it onto your belt, where you can get to it."

Pat gave me a sad smile. "Bad vibes were getting me this morning. I was thinking the same. I'd not like to use it, but I have to agree, best be ready, not sorry."

She found a no-parking-from-here-to-corner slot two streets away from Menard's and backed the Mustang in while I called the local precinct. I told the dispatcher our location, with an instruction to keep uniformed officers away.

"You called a code five, but we're not on an undercover stakeout," said Pat.

"No, but it keeps everybody away and cuts down on tickets. The police card on the dash doesn't work in all districts. In some areas, it even gets your car vandalized."

We walked up the hill to Menard's address. The house was a 1920s red-brick mansion. All the wood sills, shutters, and trim were a well-maintained, immaculate white. The fancy wrought-iron gate was closed but not locked. I pushed it open, and we strolled up the flagstone walk as if we owned the place.

"They don't build 'em like that anymore," I said.

"Ah, now, welcome to the good life," Pat said, doing a little curtsy.

I punched the doorbell six times before getting an answer. A fiftyish sourpuss opened the door. She had pasty skin and a thin, straight mouth that looked as if it would shatter if she were ever to smile. Her simple mid-length maroon dress and the white frilly collar around her skinny neck announced her to be the maid.

"Good morning, we need to talk to Monique Menard," I said.

She shook her head at me. "We are not expecting anyone. It's way too early. Come back later."

I flipped out the badge an inch from her nose. "No, I don't think so."

The stone-faced maid led us through a mirrored foyer into a large but cozy living room. The space was zoned into two U-shaped conversation islands made up of long rectangular sofas and double-wide chairs. A collection of ornate framed watercolors, depicting landmarks of Montreal and Quebec City, adorned the left of the room. I recognized one by John Collins, who was more famous for his editorial cartoons in the Montreal Gazette than his streetscapes. Also, a William

Morris. On the right, a triple-glazed glass wall opened to a view of a mountainside park.

"Please be seated," said Sourpuss. "I will advise Miss Menard of your presence."

I plopped down across from Pat, a ten-foot river of sculpted designer carpet separating us. It alone probably cost more than all the furnishings in my apartment.

Twenty minutes later, we were still waiting. My fingers drummed a countdown on the chair arm. Mere seconds before I was about to start throwing my weight around, Miss Menard finally made her appearance. She walked in, her hips swaying hello, her long blond hair swishing with the beat. She wore a light-blue semitransparent negligee that showed off most of her not-entirely-organic assets. I stood up to greet her. She ignored me and slunk on past to drape herself artfully on one of the chairs, tossing a silver-colored high-heeled slipper off with a flick of her toes and then tucking her bare foot under her.

"Why do you police people have to do everything so early?" she moaned. "It's barely eleven."

"Do you know a Diana James?" I asked.

She gave Pat a sideways-under-the-lashes glance and said to me, "Why do you want to know?"

"Okay, let's try again. Do you know Diana James?"

Menard rolled her eyes and looked up at the ceiling. "If you have to know, she's a close friend of mine. Why are you are asking me these questions?"

"Her car was parked downtown in Old Montreal and—"

She cut me off in mid sentence, sticking out her hand, her manicured fingers brushing the air as if to wipe inconsequential me out of her important life.

"Diana's car is always getting towed or ticketed. She just parks it anywhere. It doesn't seem to bother her one bit. I'm sure she'll take care of the fine; it's really no big deal. Why are you bothering me with this?"

My leg had fallen asleep as my impatience awoke. I lifted my imposing bulk from her elegant cream-colored microfiber chair. My right foot was half numb. The pinpricks of renewed circulation tingled up my leg as I closed the distance between us.

My wide frame cut off the morning sun streaming in from the floor-to-ceiling windows behind me. From that angle, my shadow appeared to be the only thing covering the pouting woman in front of me. Two alluring spots of pink stared boldly at me through the flimsy nightie. I cleared my throat and, with some effort, lifted my gaze to her eyes. "What I tried to tell you is that we found her BMW in a parking lot close to Old Montreal. Unfortunately, we also found her body in the trunk."

She jerked her head back as if I had slapped her. She began breathing in little gasps and blinking rapidly, as if refocusing her eyes would make both me and the horrid news go away. Her salon-tanned face lost some of its color, and tears began to stream over the remnants of last night's mascara.

She had annoyed me with her attitude, so maybe I was a tad tough on her. Now I stood surprised to see her cool exterior cracking fast, like thin ice under an overweight skater.

"Ah, eh, I guess you can take a minute to compose yourself," I mumbled.

Pat moved in, shooing me away. "Robert, I swear, you must have graduated from the Attila the Hun school of interpersonal relations," she said. "Miss Menard, I'm Sergeant Patricia O'Neil. Please excuse Lieutenant Beaudry. If he doesn't get his coffee in the morning, it makes him a grumpy bear."

The eavesdropping maid had a sudden attack of courtesy and offered me a cup. Pat pointed to the kitchen with a nod of her head. I didn't need to be a detective to recognize a womanly ploy to get me out of the room.

It took Pat a full forty minutes to calm Menard before we could continue the interview.

TWENTY

Pat sat on the sofa close to Menard, and I sat on the chair opposite. The poor woman was all cried out. The tears had dried, but her breathing gushed out in little hiccups and she talked in staccato bursts.

"We haven't—dating—long," she stuttered. "This Saturday w-would, have been our ten-month-aversary."

"I'm really sorry, Monique," I said. "Maybe I was a bit brusque earlier. We interviewed her store employees. They only said good things about her. I promise we'll find out who did this."

Menard looked me in the eyes to see if I was telling the truth. I gave her my most delicate smile and put my smartphone on the coffee table.

"I'll record the interview. You may be a material witness in the case, and it's important that we get your story straight," I continued.

"Was Diana part of Starlight Modeling?" Pat asked.

"No-no. I do modeling, and I have the Quebec franchise for the group. I recruit the models for my branch of the agency myself. Diana h-had her store. She didn't like my career."

Pat moved closer and took Monique's hand. "We know all about Starlight, dear. Where're not here for that."

Menard dropped her head and slumped lower into the sofa. "We met at Pink's. It—it was as if we had known each other for years. The next weekend, we flew to Paris. It was so—so romantic." The tears welled up again.

Pat put her arm around the grieving madam's shoulder. It calmed her.

"When were you last with Diana?" I said.

"We spent the weekend up north, at a friend's country place. Then we went to a big party Monday evening at a fishing lodge farther north. We came back to Montreal late Tuesday afternoon. Diana stayed here that night, and we had breakfast together the next morning."

"She hasn't called you since then?" I said.

"No. In—in fact, she forgot her cell phone here on the charger Wednesday morning. She took a million pictures at the party. Her battery was dead."

Pat looked at me, her lips forming an "O," as in "Bingo!"

"We're going to need Diana's phone," I said. "Those pictures may be important."

Menard's eyes filled again, and her voice quavered. "Does her murder have something to do with me . . . or with Starlight?"

"Monique, at this point we don't know," Pat said. "I'm sure that none of this was your fault at all, at all." She took both Menard's hands. "I know this is difficult for you, but I need you to be strong. We really need your help."

Menard stopped snuffling but clung to Pat's hands like someone neck deep in quicksand.

Menard told us that the party was at the fishing lodge of a well-known Montreal city councillor. She added that he was a regular patron of Starlight's, and indiscreetly mentioned some of his fetishes to us.

"'Spank-Spank, Kiss-Kiss,' we named him. We met him by chance in a restaurant in Mont-Tremblant Saturday evening. He invited us to a big bash he was having for a bunch of very rich and influential people. He said we would dress up the party, no strings attached. Diana was hesitant, but I told him yes. We really enjoyed ourselves."

She continued with details of the party, pausing at moments to resume her crying jag.

On Monday afternoon, they had met their host at the restaurant and then driven to his fishing lodge in a big four-by-four truck. Monique had a good memory. She gave me detailed directions to the councillor's country place. Somewhere during these recollections, the sourpuss maid brought me Diana's cell phone.

By the end of our interview, Menard was exhausted and emptied of tears. She was too weak in the knees to walk. Pat and the maid helped her wobble up the stairs to her bedroom, and I went into the hallway and called our boss.

"Pat and I just finished questioning Diana James's girlfriend, Monique Menard. We're still here at her place. I think the killer may have been after some pictures Diana took with her cell phone. On Monday evening, she was at a party up north, past Mont-Tremblant. Apparently, there were a lot of rich and influential bigwigs at this get-together, and Diana took a lot of pictures. The good news is that I have her cell phone in my hand. The bad news is that one of our better-known city councilmen hosted the party and he's a regular customer of the Starlight rent-a-girl club. He likes to play the professor spanking the naughty schoolgirl."

I gave him the councillor's name.

"I'd like to interview him and get the list of guests from the party," I said.

"Aw, rats!" Jean growled. "He's one of our more vocal police supporters, and he's on the police ethics committee. I can't believe this! Beaudry, you have a knack for opening cans of worms that everyone would just as soon stayed shut. I don't want you to question the councillor in your usual Genghis Khan diplomatic style. I can smell trouble already. I'm going to call him first and have a private conversation, man to man.

Don't do anything concerning him before I talk to you. Don't even go near him."

"Nice to have your vote of confidence, Jean," I said breezily.

"I'm protecting you from yourself, Beaudry, because I do have confidence in your ability to get to the bottom of things, come hell or high water. For once, please just do it my way."

"Okay, boss. I'm cool. We'll pass by the office to give the cell phone to Dobson. I need those pictures printed. We need to identify all of the guests."

Jean hung up as Pat joined me in the foyer.

"You should see Monique's walk-in closet," she said. "It's the size of my old living room. She's got a wall of shoes like you have a wall of books. And she protects her shoes fierce. The closet door is dead-bolted to the floor and ceiling and steel plated on the inside."

The maid came down the stairs from Monique's room to tell us she would see us out. I was surprised to see her mouth curled in a little smile, and her face hadn't cracked at all. I turned in front of her and blocked her path to the front door.

"Are you a live-in maid?" I said. "Does Miss Menard have someone here twenty-four hours a day?"

The maid crossed her arms in front of her chest and began tapping an impatient drumbeat with her right foot. "Don't worry," she said, "we'll take good care of Monique. I'll make sure of that. Our doors are always locked, and there's always someone here. When we have guests in the evening, we have a security man who acts as the butler. During the day, if I'm out grocery shopping, the gardener takes my place in the house."

"I don't want to frighten you," I said. "There's a chance that Diana's killer may want to get to Monique as well. It would be best if Miss Menard didn't leave the house unless absolutely necessary—at least for the next few days, until we get this sorted out. If I can, I'll have a patrol car posted to watch the house."

The maid went down the hall and opened a closet a few feet from where we were standing. Clipped to the inside of the door was a short-barreled Mossberg 500 shotgun with pistol grip and a folding stock that held extra shells. Not exactly your standard housecleaning equipment.

She looked at me, her eyes cold and hard. "Do I look frightened to you, Lieutenant?" "Maybe you should be. This guy's a pro. You'd better know your way around that twelve-gauge. He won't be handing out second chances."

The maid maintained her stern look and nodded toward the door.

TWENTY-ONE

Bathed in the delicate warmth of a noon spring sun, we walked down the hill from Monique Menard's house. The birds were rioting and the squirrels, squirreling, and not a cloud was in the sky. I felt content. We were finally getting somewhere with the case. It was going to be a good day.

"We have to drop off Diana's phone to Dobson," I said. "Why don't we grab a bite down the street from headquarters? I know a great spot in Chinatown. It's such a beautiful day, I think that after lunch we should drive up north and scout our party giver's country place."

Pat agreed with the plan, unaware of her uncle's warnings and admonitions to me regarding not going near to the councillor. We reached the intersection at the bottom of the hill, and a fresh breeze carried the scent of baking bread from a little corner dépanneur.

Across the street, some guy jumped up and down on the hood of Pat's Mustang. A passing mailman looked wide-eyed at the scene, gave me a Gallic shrug, and continued on his way.

"Mark, ya gobshite!" Pat shrieked.

Intent on getting her hands on him, she bounded off the curb and into the path of an oncoming delivery truck. In a move worthy of Jackie Chan or maybe Bruce Lee, I pivoted on the ball of one foot, snatched her collar and yanked her backward. The truck's front tire passed an inch from the toes of her pointy boots. In my right hand, I held a long bit of thread, the label from her suede jacket, and a fistful of red hair, which, happily, was still attached to my indignant but otherwise unscathed partner.

The two-ton screeched to a halt, filling the air with the smell of burned rubber, along with the sharp clink of breaking glassware from the shifting load in its cargo area. The bald, portly driver jumped out of the cab like a jack-in-the-box, both tattooed arms flailing in a fair imitation of a Pinocchio worked by an intoxicated puppeteer. His first words were liberally punctuated with French epithets having to do with a mentally challenged female dog of uncertain lineage.

I walked up, and before he could utter his next string of profanities, my badge flashed in front of his face.

"Get back in your truck and move it—now."

The marionette stopped gesticulating and dropped its arms as if someone suddenly cut the strings.

Muttering under his breath, he climbed back into the driver's seat and slammed the door.

By the time the transport shifted out of the way and Pat got her heart going again, Mark had disappeared into his tan Mercedes-AMG and peeled away from the next street corner. I helped a wobbly-legged Pat cross the street to her damaged car.

"It's drivable," I said. "Only a flesh wound. One smashed headlight, and you'll need a new hood—this one looks like a casualty from a buffalo stampede."

Pat ran her hand along the scratches and dents. She shook her head. "That's it—I'm uninsurable. My broker is Japanese. He's going to commit hara-kiri, for sure."

I pointed to the damage. "I can see that your ex is truly demented. But I have to say, he dances a mean flamenco. I did like the little twirl at the end."

"Ara be whist, you big oaf! Don't even try and make me laugh. This is nawful!"

"Did you cancel your antitheft GPS tracking device?" I said.

"Ah, shite, I'm a real omadhaun. I totally forgot!"

"Call the installer and put an end to Mark's little game," I said. "Let's sit in the car and make a few calls."

Pat phoned the GPS tracking service. By the time she finished, Mark was off the access list, and they had apologized profusely and given her two years of free service. While she was laying into the customer service people, I called a cousin of Nico's at Midnight Auto

Parts and Repair. It didn't bother me that they changed addresses every three months or so. They were cheap, and they were fast.

"Don't bother your insurance company," I said. "I've arranged a fast repair for your bruised Mustang, and a loaner. It's on our way downtown."

"That's bleedin' deadly," said Pat.

On a roll, I put the phone on speaker and made another call, this time to a friend who worked as a tax fraud investigator for the Québec revenue service.

"Revenu *Québec*, Eli Kraus speaking."

"Good morning, Eli, it's Bob Beaudry. We're past due for a good lunch together, but you have to do me a small favor first."

"You don't have to bribe me with food," he said. "Anything for you, Bobby."

"I just want to give you a hot lead. The name Mark Weston came up in one of our investigations. We know he's a slimy lawyer who specializes in tax-evasion tricks for his clients. At the moment, we can't nab him for anything, but maybe from your end?"

"Not to worry," Eli said. "I'll spearhead a surprise audit myself. We'll take him and his clients apart piece by piece. I'll give you feedback next week when I take you up on the big lunch offer. In the meantime, I'll be working up an appetite."

Before we hung up, Pat gave him Mark's office address, phone numbers, and a short list of a few of the shadier schemes that her ex-husband had been imprudent enough to boast about.

Pat looked at me, her mouth straight and her eyes serious. "When I applied for homicide," she said, "I wasn't sure I would like the job. I'm still not sure. But I'm sure of one thing: I really like you, Big Bear. You're special."

I wasn't certain what she meant by "special," only that I liked the sound of it.

"You're blushing," I said. "I'll take that as a lopsided Irish compliment. The tax people are going to give Mark a full-fledged, no-gel proctology exam. I guarantee he won't have time to bother you for a while."

"I hope so," Pat said as she started her battered car.

TWENTY-TWO

We left Nico's cousin's shop, driving a nearly new four-door Jeep Wrangler. Pat spent several minutes adjusting the seat height, seat back rake, steering wheel angle, and exterior mirror angles and then drove us to headquarters.

The balmy weather all but begged us to be outside. Downtown sidewalks were filled with office workers and store clerks hurrying back from lunch. The pedestrians, looking down at the sidewalk or straight ahead, took scant notice of the lovely weather. They didn't seem to appreciate that the sad gray winter skies were now a happier light blue.

* * *

At headquarters, Pat went to see Uncle Jean about getting some protection around Monique Menard's house. I went to the tech section's floor to meet with Dobson. I found him at a workstation cubicle at the end of the office, typing like a legal secretary stuck pounding out a last-minute brief before dashing off to happy hour. His computer display was an array three monitors wide. Documents flipped from one screen to another as he worked.

"Fancy setup," I said.

"You guys get the guns; we get the toys," Dobson said.

"I said the same thing to Pat a few hours ago. This is our victim Diana's phone. She took pictures at a party last Monday. I need prints of the photos, and identities of the people in the pictures. I think the killer or killers were looking for these pictures when they tossed Diana's house. This phone just may be our Rosetta stone."

Dobson glanced at the phone, pulled out a tangle of wires from under his desk, and plugged one into it. A minute and a few keystrokes later, he had the phone's contents downloaded and on-screen.

"Not that many guests at the party," he said. "We have twenty or so different faces, once or several times in the sequence. It looks as if most of the pictures were taken on the fly, without the subject knowing. Few people are actually looking at the camera. None of the pictures appear posed, and many of the frames are out of focus. I'll need to do a bit of work on this."

"Look at that heaped buffet table," I said. "Replete with an ice carving of a horn of plenty. The few guests present at the party should have had enough to eat for a week or more."

We examined each of the snapshots. Neither Dobson nor I recognized anyone. Although Monique Menard had said our illustrious city councillor was hosting the party, he was conspicuously missing from Diana's impromptu photo shoot.

"I'll clean up the blurry shots, sharpen and enhance all of them," Dobson said. "Then I'll pull out and crop each person individually. I can then run the series through the CRPQ/CIP police information database and see if we get a hit from the facial-recognition software."

"Great," I said. "When you're done, can you e-mail a copy of the pictures to my phone?"

Dobson assured me he would take care of everything technical, and I left him to do his computer magic. On my way out the door, he said to be sure and say hello to Pat for him.

I met up her in the main-floor lobby.

"I'll spare you the budget speech and other excuses my uncle gave me," Pat said. "The bottom line is that Menard is on her own. She gets no police protection."

"Disappointed but not surprised," I said.

Pat shrugged and then made a spooning motion in front of her mouth. "Munch-munch time?"

"Yeah. I'm hungry, too. You're in for a treat. My secret Chinese restaurant is just a step away from our parking lot. It's on St-Laurent, above Chinatown and below the trendy north section. The food's always fresh. If you like it, we could come back on a Saturday evening. They present a floor show of sorts. The cooks come out into the restaurant and make their own noodles in front of the patrons."

Pat pointed to the door. "You take the lead, partner, and I'll back you up."

I stepped ahead but then stood back to open the door for her. Women want to be treated on equal terms as men, but they still appreciate some chivalry. That made me realize, I had just asked Pat out on a date with my Saturday-evening-at-the-restaurant comment. I wasn't sure whether I had just made a faux pas. She hadn't said yes or no, and I hadn't caught any telltale facial cue. It was getting more difficult to see Pat as just a work partner. I pushed aside my feelings as we headed outside.

TWENTY-THREE

Pat was driving the Jeep, and I was doing navigation. The afternoon had warmed up nicely, and I dialed the air-conditioning to a tad cooler, to fight the drowsiness from our overeating. After our Chinese lunch, the seat belts seemed to fit a bit tighter around our middles. Pat turned onto Highway 15 north. I figured it was at least a two-hour drive to the Laurentian Mountains.

Ten minutes later, the traffic started to bog down to a solid stream, four lanes wide, of American and Japanese steel and plastic, with a few high-end German models sprinkled in here and there. Drivers were squirming in their seats as the parade slowed by another five miles an hour.

"It's two thirty in the afternoon!" I said. "Where do all these people come from? And where can they be going? Doesn't anybody work? What happened to nine to five?"

"It's Friday," Pat said. "People leave earlier. Look. I see emergency-vehicle lights blinking up ahead. It'll clear up after that, I'm sure. Don't be impatient. You're not driving anyway, so just enjoy the ride. By the by, Robert, I'm always driving. Are you going to get yourself a new car?"

"Since the GTO, I haven't summoned the will to hunt for something I would really like. Maybe I have some type of psychological block."

"Oh, maybe I shoud'na mentioned that. Me and me big yap. I'm a blathering eejit sometimes."

"No, quite the contrary. You've been a breath of fresh air. I'm even beginning to figure out some of your Dublin vocabulary."

I examined the Wrangler's interior finish. It was equipped with a six-CD player and a few other high-tech gadgets, but no navigation system.

"Nice rig," I said. "Looks square and chunky outside, but it's quite plush inside. How does it drive?"

Pat put her left hand up on the roll cage above the door.

"It's chunky inside, too—there's these padded tube things all around. It feels secure and solid, and I like that we're higher, and with the big outside mirrors, I can see well all around. It drives smooth, but stiffer than my Mustang—slower, too."

The density of cars began to thin as we headed farther north. By the time we passed Mont-Tremblant and its famous ski village complex, we had the road nearly to ourselves. The phone service had been intermittent since entering the mountainous region an hour north of Montreal. I put my smartphone on the dashboard for better reception. It helped some, but a few miles past Tremblant, the display went to zero bars and stayed there. But the TomTom GPS application I was running on the screen seemed to function even without cellular service. I didn't question the technology.

A few miles back, the highway had narrowed to a winding two-lane road. The temperature had dropped a bit since we left Montreal. We were now officially off the beaten track and headed into the wilds of northern Quebec. We went around another bend. Up ahead, a white road sign advised us pictorially to slow down to a more sedate town speed. The next sign announced our arrival in the village of Labelle.

"Okay, take the next right to the town center," I said, "and then it'll be another right to the bridge. We cross the river, then head north up a small road toward Little Caribou Lake. The map shows the turnoff on your side. Watch for the signs."

Ten minutes later, we turned left onto an unpaved road. This far north, spring was still on the way. Even in mid-April, snow patches covered the ground on the north side of trees and hills. The road, though clear of ice, was muddy and cut across here and there by small runoff streams flowing down from the mountains on our left. The Jeep took the ruts, puddles, and stream crevasses in stride.

The GPS map showed the cabin we were looking for on the lakeside, less than a half mile to our right. It couldn't be far, but the trees and underbrush were so dense that even with bare winter branches and few evergreens, we couldn't see more than twenty feet into the gray, twisted growth.

The Jeep lurched over a hump and splashed through another mud puddle, and my phone bounced off the dashboard. I saved it with a lucky left-hand catch. Pat glanced sideways at me, smiled, and backed off the gas a notch.

"Good for me we don't have my Mustang today," she said. "I wouldn't need Mark to destroy it—this bleedin' road alone would do it."

"That problem is behind you," I said. "Forget the bum."

"Thanks again. And fair game to you."

I pointed ahead of us. "Speaking of game, those marks in the mud ahead look like bear tracks. Our councillor takes privacy to a whole other level. If Menard hadn't given me such a good description of her trip up from Tremblant, his country lair would be near impossible to find."

At the next bend, a wider graveled road, identified by a small sign with the number "12," led toward the lakeside. Fifty feet farther down stood a guard shack with a large "Private Road" sign nailed to it.

"Number twelve," I said. "That's what Monique told us. Don't stop; pass it by. There's another parallel road up ahead. We'll turn into there."

The parallel road was just a logging trail. I told Pat to stop and put the Jeep in four-wheel drive. We found a flat, dry spot to one side, and she maneuvered the truck around so that we faced back out toward the road. I got out and walked behind the Jeep to guide as Pat backed up deeper into the forest. When we were far enough not to be seen from the roadside, she stopped, and I walked back around to the driver's side. Pat opened the door but didn't step out.

"I'm a Dublin girl," she said. "My idea of a walk in the wild is crossing St. Stephen's Green on a Sunday morning. You're not getting me to traipse in a muddy forest full of bears. I'm not dressed nor have the shoes for it."

I laughed. "Okay, city girl. I have to admit, those cute little high-heel suede boots may not be ideal, but you don't have to worry—one track does not a forest full of ravening bears make. It probably went to scout the lake and back to its den for a snooze. The trees and bushes up here are a couple of weeks later on the budding calendar than their more southerly Montreal relations. No budding greenery, no spring shoots, no food, no bruins."

"Fine," she said. "How about this: I'll wait here and commune visually with nature while you go play wilderness scout."

I tucked my jeans into my Tony Lama boots, picked up an alder branch that would do for a walking stick, and headed into thick woods.

TWENTY-FOUR

Ten feet into the bush, I located a tall pine tree. To aid in identifying it as my base marker, I made a pile of earth and leaf litter on its forest side and piled a bunch of dead boughs into a three-foot-high cone that clearly looked manmade.

Then I used my wristwatch as a compass. It was just about five in the afternoon. I held the watch horizontally and pointed the hour hand at the sun, using the midpoint between the four and the twelve to locate south. I sighted over the two o'clock position and estimated that the country house was due east from where I stood.

I walked carefully into the forest, avoiding gullies and low muddy spots. Zigzagging to keep to higher ground, I kept an easterly heading toward the councillor's house. I got lucky and crossed a game trail heading toward the lake. There I scrounged more dead branches to make a large arrow pointing back to my own trail and start point. I followed the narrow rut for fifteen minutes or so before I could see the lake through the branches.

Coming out of the woods at the water's edge, I heard the chug of a diesel engine up ahead. I followed the shoreline until I saw a roof ridge peeking above a low rise on my right. The hill was high enough to hide the rest of the house from view. I crept up the rise on all fours and then belly-crawled behind a scraggly evergreen. I stayed for a few minutes, listening for any signs of life, before edging over to look at the house. The motor kept chugging away. I heard no other sound.

I looked into the clearing in front of me. This was no mere cabin in the woods: a hotel-size main lodge with other buildings clustered around. It looked more like a military compound than a country estate.

On the downslope of the rise, a perimeter fence topped with razor wire protected the property. The large two-story log house that Menard described faced the road. From my position, the view was of the rear windowed balcony, facing the lake. The big log house was flanked by two windowless single-story buildings with gabled roofs, resembling low barns. They were offset to the side and rear of the main house. Two hundred feet from my position along the lake's edge was a boathouse. On the top of the boathouse on the lake side, a small wood-and-canvas cupola had been built. It was empty. The diesel engine noise came from the direction of the boathouse. Someone must be in there working.

The house's wide balcony was empty. There didn't seem to be anyone around. I crawled back down from the rise, then, in a low crouch, followed a four-foot-high fieldstone retaining wall that ran along the lakeshore to the boathouse. The engine sound was coming from around front.

Slipping over the wall, I crawled along the side of the boathouse and braved a glance around the corner. A fair-size generator was mounted on a concrete pad, covered by a lean-to extension of the boathouse. Here, away from the main house, it could provide the electricity for the complex while minimizing the noise for the guests. If it was running, people were present somewhere in the compound.

From my new vantage point, I could see four big three-wheeled ATVs and two larger eight-balloon-tire amphibious models, all parked in a line along the left barn building. One of the ATVs sported a gun rack with what looked like a Heckler & Koch 400-series assault rifle strapped into it. That certainly wasn't kosher, as my friend Eli Kraus would have said. Canada has some of the strictest gun laws in North America, and assault rifles were definitely not on the list of approved hunting tools.

I inched open a side door of the boathouse. There was no boat, only a large snowmobile partly covered by a tarpaulin. A rack on a side wall held ten forty-gallon diesel-oil drums. In a corner, I found two empty metal ammunition boxes. If these people bought ammo by the case, they were probably honing their shooting skills. They must have a shooting range set up somewhere in the barnlike buildings. I figured that when facing an unknown number of armed strangers, discretion would get me better results than my usual frontal attack, which would present them with a wide, easy target. Intent on a fast exit, I slipped back out of the boathouse, in a crouch.

I paused outside and took a few pictures of the compound with my cell phone. Before I finished my little snapshot survey, a door opened on the side of the main house. Luckily, it swung toward the lake, which gave me the fraction of a second I needed to flatten out in the shadow of the boathouse before a man came into view. Not an easy feat when you're my size. I felt the wet earth seep into my jeans as I lay motionless. The man carried a tall aluminum container with both hands. I smelled the coffee from fifty feet downwind. He was under six feet, dark skinned, with little rimless glasses perched on a doozy of a hooked nose. He wore deep-forest camo fatigue pants, a black cable-knit sweater, and a black watch cap. A semiautomatic pistol in a web holster was strapped to his right leg. He headed away from me, walking along the barn structure to my right, and disappeared from view as he turned the corner toward the front of the building. I sprinted out of my hole and jumped down behind the retaining wall, keeping an eye on the guy. He yelled a command as he turned toward the front of the barn. The language was guttural, and I couldn't make it out—definitely not French or English.

Thinking he may have spotted me, I froze in place and eased my gun out. A few long seconds later, I heard him kick at the door. I presumed that with his hands full, he just wanted someone to open up for him. I slid my weapon back under my arm as someone from inside opened the door for the Nose. Over to my left, behind the second barn structure, I heard a car engine start. I peeked over the wall. A black Hummer with two men aboard headed away from the house, toward the entrance road. The driver had a full beard and long hair; the passenger was bald. They fit George's description of Diana's killers. I had what I needed. It was time to get my butt out of here—no sense in pushing my luck. I turned and followed the stone wall back to the edge of the woods, took a fast compass bearing, and, as quietly as I could, hiked back toward Pat and the Jeep.

A few minutes into the bush, I heard what sounded like one of the ATVs firing up. Good—the noise would mask the crackle of my footsteps on twigs and dry leaves, letting me pick up my pace. Even better, the trail I was on was too narrow for the ATVs I had seen. Worried that the Hummer and the ATV were on patrol and might find Pat alone in our car, I double-timed it for the logging trail.

The sun was about to set when I spotted my reference pine tree. I came out of the woods two car lengths in front of the Jeep. Pat leaped out of the car, ran to me, and jumped up to put her arms around my neck. Stunned, I undid her grasp and held her at arm's length. Her eyes were red, as if she had been crying.

"Are you okay?" I said.

"You big oaf, you've been gone hours! I thought a wild animal ate you!"

"Don't be silly," I said. "The most dangerous thing in that forest was me."

Pat punched me hard on the shoulder, told me I smelled like leaf mold, and stomped back to the passenger side of the car. I got in, took her left hand, and apologized—I wasn't sure just what for, but it seemed the right thing to do.

"It's okay, it's okay," she said. "Just get us out of here."

It was already dusk and hard to see on the trail, even with the driving lights on. Crawling the Jeep forward in low, I fiddled with the multiposition light switch until I found the notch for the bumper spotlights. That did the trick. They put the ground in front of us in broad daylight. We came off the logging trail, and I turned left toward the village.

When we were abreast of the entrance to the encampment, I saw the black Hummer parked at the guardhouse, with the bald guy and the bearded guy in it. As we passed them, the truck's lights came on, and the driver turned onto the road to the village and followed behind us. They stayed ten or twelve car lengths back until we were close to the village bridge, where the street lighting began. The Hummer then dropped back to twenty car lengths.

I slowed the Jeep and hugged the right side of the road. "We're being followed," I said.

Pat said her first words since we got in the Jeep. "I know; the passenger took a picture."

I slowed and turned into the parking lot of a saloon-type bar. I slipped my arm around Pat's her shoulders and whispered in her ear. "Let's pretend we're just lovers who've been making out far from prying eyes."

"You wish," Pat said.

"Maybe," I said.

As the Hummer approached, I bent toward her and gave her a delicate pretend kiss on the lips. I was pleasantly bewildered when she responded more passionately. The Hummer slowed to a crawl while passing us, then turned onto a side street. We broke our lip lock, and I put the Jeep back into gear as if nothing had happened. I didn't leave her time to speak, nor did I comment on her surprisingly affectionate kiss. I immediately started telling her about my trek in the woods. I gave her the details about the councillor's military-style encampment. She asked a few questions but, for the most part, was strangely quiet.

We made better time on the way back to Montreal, reaching my house at nine p.m. sharp. When we turned into my street, Pat said, "You just passed a beige or silver Buick Lucerne. It has a Hertz rental sticker on the bumper, and two tough-looking chaps on board. As we went by, they dropped down in their seats, trying to avoid being seen."

"I must be getting old," I said. "I missed that. I'll drive on by; let's see what they do."

The Buick's lights turned on as they started the car. I turned left at the next intersection and slowed. A second later, the Buick turned in behind us.

"That's another brownie point for you, Sherlock," I said. "Let's see how good they are at follow the leader."

I turned right, cranked up the Jeep's big V-6, and turned right again, ignoring a stop sign, then turned left with more speed and the same disregard of traffic laws. I took a main boulevard at twenty miles per hour above the limit.

"Your grand prix driving hasn't impressed them much at all," Pat said.

The Buick was tagging along six or seven cars behind us.

"Okay," I said. "Time for the bear-behind-the-hedge trick."

After a few more fast turns, I darted into a lane behind a big hotel and slipped behind a graffiti-decorated wood panel that shielded the hotel's unsightly garbage container from street view. In the dark and behind the panel, we weren't visible, but I could see the street from between the slats of wood. I got a good look at the driver as they passed by in a slow search. I gave us a few minutes of wait time before firing up the Jeep.

"I'm tired and hungry," Pat said. "I hate to eat alone at the hotel. If you can be a gentleman instead of a werebear for one night, let's go to your place and order in. I'll take the couch."

"Fine with me, but the gentlebear gets the couch," I said.

We were back in front of my apartment in five minutes flat.

TWENTY-FIVE

The chef at Trattoria Milano, a small family restaurant a block west from my apartment, was a friend of mine. He sent one of his waiters to personally deliver our chicken marsala and fettucine.

"A feast for a king and queen," I said.

The big paper bag contained the main course, two insalata mista in plastic containers, a loaf of fresh-baked bread, and a box of cannoli.

"It smells yummy," Pat said. "But methinks the dessert is four hundred calories all by itself."

"Right you are," I said. "Sergio's homemade cannoli are four hundred calories, per bite."

Crackers jumped onto the table, sniffed our meal, jumped back down, and trotted over to the patio door, where he meowed to be let out.

"He likes the meatballs and ravioli, but nothing else Italian is on his list," I said.

Pat moved a few feet, bent down to pet Crackers, then slid the patio door open for him.

"By the way, while you were ordering I re-potted your fern," Pat said.

My crazy cat had won his longstanding feud with the Boston fern in my living room. Earlier, when we had stepped into the apartment, we discovered an empty flowerpot and a trail of loose earth down the hallway to the kitchen, where the remnants of the Nephrolepis exaltata lay in disarray beside his empty food bowl.

I opened a bottle of Nero D'avola and decanted it while Pat set the table. She moved quietly and slowly as if lost in a daydream, her mind not in the moment and not focused on what she was actually doing. We sat at my little kitchen table, facing each other. I told her about some of the more bizarre antics that Crackers had performed in the past year, and she nodded and smiled but said little. I let her enjoy the food and stopped talking.

After our little feast, I made us each a cup of tea, and we went to sit side by side on the living-room sofa.

"Are you all right?" I asked. "You've been strangely quiet tonight. Did I do something wrong?"

Pat shook her head. "No, Big Bear, it's not you. You've been great. This homicide business is a bit more intense than the fraud squad. And my divorce hearing is next week. Just a lot of stuff in the old noggin, I guess."

"I can empathize with that. I've had a hard winter, and on the next calendar page I turn forty. Compared to me, half the people I work with are young kids. My noggin is also a bit fuzzy. In the same month, I lost a wife and earned a suspension for behaving violently with a team of bank robbers. I'm still trying to sort out what I could have done differently in both cases."

"Jean told me about that," she said. "The consensus on the hostage scene was that the gurriers appeared to be off with the fairies. They didn't leave you much choice. My uncle said the political pressure was from Internal Affairs. Apparently, you've been fast on the trigger before."

"Some cops go to retirement without ever having unholstered their weapon. But I seem to attract gunplay," I said. "It generally gets me in the crosshairs of Internal Affairs. For it to be a justified use of force, I have to be saving someone's life. So far, I've always had a good case. I guess it makes the IA guys lose face."

"When I was on patrol in Dublin, we carried a baton and Mace but no firearm," Pat said. "Only the special squads carry guns. It's different here—the brigands generally have more firepower than us."

"You're not kidding. One of those bank robbers carried an AK-forty-seven, the others had Magnum revolvers. They were too far gone on speed, or whatever recreational chemical they had pumped into themselves, to listen to reason. I told them that the only way for them to leave on their feet was that there had to be no violence. Unfortunately, a female teller felt faint and sat down suddenly. One of the robbers turned and shot her in the hip. So I shot all three of them—didn't want 'em shooting her again."

"When the bullets are flying fast and furious, we react the way we were trained," Pat said. "That's all you did."

"I've never told anyone this. I went wild when he shot her. In my mind, he had shot Colleen, not the teller. When I realized that they were all down, it scared me. I felt I went off the deep end for a minute."

Pat took my hand in both of hers and said, "Robert, you—"

My phone sang its tune from the kitchen counter. The moment was lost.

"You'd best get that," Pat said, releasing my hand.

I dragged myself to the kitchen, picked up the phone, and answered. My boss's voice assailed my ear.

"Where the hell have you been? I've tried calling you all afternoon!"

"My battery died," I lied. "It's back charging now."

"I couldn't get hold of our councillor. He's in France on business and won't be back until Monday. It wasn't time for you to pull a vanishing act. All hell's broken loose. I've had a parade of law enforcement agencies with initials and no names—RCMP, CSIS, CBSA—harassing me since three this afternoon. The pictures you asked Dobson to send to the police information center have stirred up a hornets' nest."

"Who have they identified?" I said.

"I don't know—nobody's telling me anything. 'National security' is the excuse they're using to pull the case from us. They want to talk to you."

"Don't worry," I said. "I'll find out what gives."

"Beaudry, when you say 'don't worry,' it's time to pack the chinaware. Do not—I repeat, do not—get yourself or the department in trouble. You find out anything, get back to me immediately if not sooner."

"O-o-ka-a-ay, boss."

Jean hung up, and I said to Pat, "We were right. One of Diana's pictures was dynamite. The RCMP and the CSIS spooks are invoking national security to try and take the case from us."

"We have two murders in our jurisdiction," she said. "They can't do that."

"Don't worry, we'll fight it tooth and nail," I said.

"My teeth and nails are a little tired tonight. How about we save the fight for tomorrow?"

I took the hint and went to put clean sheets on my bed. I was coming back to the living room with a few blankets for my night on the sofa when the doorbell rang.

"Eleven twenty in the evening? You've got an active life, Robert. Do you want me to answer the door?"

I sidestepped into the kitchen. The driver of the Buick that tailed us earlier that evening appeared on my door-monitor screen.

"No, get back here," I said. "Our followers from this evening are at the door."

I pressed the button to open the front door. It opened slowly, and a bald head peered carefully around the door frame.

"Lieutenant Beaudry, we're from the American embassy. We spoke to your boss, Jean O'Neil. I know it's late, but we need to talk to you."

"Come on up," I said. We like American tourists in Montreal."

They climbed the stairs, and I pointed to the living-room sofa. The bald guy said thanks, but they both remained standing.

I smiled. They looked like they were part of the same act, or at least favored the same tailor. He had matched them in identical dark-gray business suits, but to their credit, they managed to assert their individuality with differently striped ties. Maybe it was an embassy uniform. Baldy was about my height. He had a solid build and a nondescript face. He could have been an accountant or an insurance salesman. The other man's hair was salt-and-pepper and cut short. He was six feet five, very slim, but looked wiry. He carried a magazine-size black leather folder.

"Mister Beaudry, we intercepted some pictures you sent to CPIC and Nlets," he said in a gravelly voice. "We need to know how and where you got these pictures."

"You embassy guys are straight to the point," I said. "So I'll get straight to the point, too. Got any identification?"

The bald guy shook his head. "Sadly, no."

Brush Cut pointed to his partner by flipping his thumb sideways.

"He's Smith, and I'm Woods. I hear you have a tough-guy reputation, Beaudry. This is not a pissing contest. Just sit down and answer our questions."

"You've got no identification, and I've got no patience," I said. "I'm too tired to waste my time on bullshit. Now, get the hell out of my house."

Smith reached into his suit jacket, and I heard Pat's voice from the hallway behind me. "That best be your ID you're reaching for."

I stepped back a foot so I could see her and my two uninvited guests at the same time. Pat trained her weapon on the bald guy. I remembered Jean's warning that her bite was worse than her bark. I backed up a few feet to get out of her line of fire.

Smith very slowly pulled out a plasticized card and held it out at arm's length. I grabbed it with my left hand while keeping an eye on Pat. The card was a coded CIA building pass for a Mr. Irwin Parks. A picture of the bald guy was on the card.

"Say good-bye to Mr. Smith and hello to Mr. Parks," I said.

Mr. Parks took a quick sidestep and glared menacingly at Pat. She aimed at his head and thumbed off the safety on her pistol. The click got everybody's attention in the room. Mr. Brush Cut put his left hand out, palm forward, in a hold-your-horses motion. He slowly pulled a business card from his lapel pocket and handed it to Parks, who then handed it to me at arm's length. I read the card out loud.

"Michael Woods, commercial attaché, United States embassy."

Pat put the safety back on her weapon and held it down by her side. I slid the card into my shirt pocket.

"Mr. Woods, commercial attaché. At least you didn't lie about your name. But I'm not sure about your job. I had the urge to salute when you walked into the room," I said.

He stared at me for a few seconds and then cracked a thin-lipped smile. "You're right, Beaudry. A lieutenant should salute a colonel."

Pat entered the room, her gun still at her side. "Unless you boys are going to play who's-got-the-longest, mayhap we should all sit down and have a nice, collegial chat."

We all smiled at Pat, and each of us took a seat.

The spooks sat side by side on the sofa. Pat and I used the overstuffed chairs facing them. To my surprise, she put her gun between the seat cushion and the armrest—still within easy reach. Not a very trusting girl, it seemed.

"Colonel—is that Marines or Air Force?" Pat said to Woods.

Woods cracked his thin smile again. "I'm presently attached to U.S. Air Force Intelligence, ma'am."

He opened his little leather case and pulled out a set of eight-by-ten glossies, which he spread out on the coffee table facing us. They were blown-up versions of some of Diana's party pictures. He also spread out other pictures of the same people but taken in a different locales. In one of them, I could see part of a steering wheel and a car dashboard in the forefront. The subject in the picture was a heavyset man coming out of an office building. It looked typical of a surveillance photo.

Smith, aka Parks, sat impassively, but his eyes scanned continuously—not missing much, I was sure. Woods did all the talking. He pointed to Diana's picture of the buffet.

"Look in the background, behind the sculpture—those two guys talking together. The big guy is Walter Rohmer, a vice president of a well-known Swiss bank."

Woods put the surveillance photo of the same man on the left of Diana's buffet picture.

"The slim guy with the little beard he's talking to is Hamid El-Rahim. He was number six on our Most Wanted Terrorists list."

He put a mug shot of the terrorist, face front and profile, down on the table to the right of Diana's buffet picture. In this second photo, the man was clean-shaven.

"I can see that this could be a worrisome combination: big money and a known terrorist," I said.

"Particularly worrisome," Woods said, "inasmuch as El-Rahim was reported killed in Tripoli two years ago. The hit on his car was one of our first successes with the new unmanned drones. Now here he is, alive and well and stuffing his face at a party."

I nodded at Parks and Woods. "I'd love to help you find your resurrected terrorist, but I can't tell you much. We got the pictures in a search of a murder victim's apartment. We know that it was a professional hit. It's conjecture at this point, but I think your terrorist didn't want his photo circulated, and he killed her to make sure of that."

"Beaudry, I can assure you that El-Rahim didn't shoot Diana James," Woods said. "He's already left the country. We have an airport surveillance print of him in line at an Air France boarding gate. The picture was taken Tuesday morning at Pierre Elliot Trudeau Airport, so he wasn't around on Thursday, and he sure didn't run over George Banks this Friday morning."

"Good work, guys," I said. "Not only do you send me back to square one to find a new suspect, but in the same sentence you've managed to shake my faith in our airport security."

"Don't exaggerate, Beaudry," Woods said. "El-Rahim didn't ring any alarms in the computerized surveillance system, simply because his facial-recognition data was removed from the files two years ago, following his supposed demise. He's traveling with a valid French passport. Now that we know his death was faked, his face is back in the world's data banks, and a number of countries will put agents out after him. We'll get back on the trail with enough manpower to nail him sooner rather than later."

"If he's gone, then who killed Diana and poor George?" said Pat.

Woods shifted toward Pat. "Rahim never does the dirty work himself. He uses fanatics from other militant organizations or simply hires mercenaries to do his jobs. That's why he's so hard to nail: he's never around when shit happens."

"So it'll work out for both our teams. You go after your terrorist, and we go after Diana's and George's killers," I said.

For the first time, Parks spoke up. "You may think you're a tough-guy cop, Beaudry, but you're out of your league on this one. The mercenaries that El-Rahim uses aren't the type of guys that put up their hands when you yell 'Stop, police!' We need to tackle this professionally, and we don't need you or the local yokels from CSIS or the RCMP messing this up."

Woods ignored Parks's comment and continued as if he hadn't spoken. "We need all the leads we can get, Beaudry. What else have you found out?"

"Nothing, really." I looked at Pat. "We were hoping the law enforcement database would give us names to go with the pictures. All we got so far is you guys popping up with a shady Swiss banker and a terrorist. Nothing else scored a hit."

I wondered if Parks picked up on my innocent glance at Pat and realized that I wasn't going to give them the whole story. I felt that I had to add something more.

"Well, before our second victim, George Banks, was eliminated, he told us that the hit men spoke Arabic to each other. He was a vet from the first Gulf

War, so he'd know. As for Diana James, apart from a stack of parking tickets, she has a clean record. We're still backtracking through her life. I'll keep you informed if we find anything. I think she was just at the wrong place at the wrong time."

Our uninvited guests stayed another ten minutes, verbally prodding and poking with more questions about what we had found at Diana's apartment and what George had told us. Neither of us told them anything more than my original story.

I led them down to the second-floor landing, let them out, and locked the door behind them.

"When you back up your partner, you really back him up," I said.

Pat gave me a big, sleepy grin. "That's what partners do."

We both headed to our separate beds.

TWENTY-SIX

I drifted off in my old sleeping bag, under the living room skylight, looking up at the stars. The view made it feel like camping outside. I slept like a log and woke to the sound of Pat yelling at Crackers.

"Bad boy! Bad, bad, boy!"

"What atrocity did he commit this time?" I said.

"He pooped in the shower!" she yelled.

"The monster started that last winter. Sometimes, he doesn't like the feel of his litter box, and he doesn't like going outside when there's dew on the ground. There's a big green bottle of disinfectant in the center door of the vanity. Pour it all over the tiles and crank the shower up to boiling."

As I slipped into my jeans, I heard the shower start up. I launched into my tai chi routine. Somewhere between "Parting the wild horse's mane" and "Snake creeps down," Pat stepped into the kitchen. I finished my exercise and joined her at the table.

"Robert, why were you not honest with the agency guys last night? There're on the good-guys team, are they not?"

"Yes and no. I trust those two with real information as much as I'd trust a felon with my gun and wallet. I'm worried that when they find out about Monique Menard, they'll spread the word that she has the pictures—use her as bait to flush out associates of El-Rahim. If they capture any of his team, they'll make them disappear. They won't read them their rights and question them politely downtown, the way we do. And that means we'll never get to find out who killed Diana or George, and our case will stay open forever. I don't blame them for wanting to get another terrorist, but not at the cost of Monique and, probably, her hard-assed maid. And not at the cost of leaving a murder case unsolved on our watch."

"I'm after telling you! You may be right about the spy guys. Now I'm nervous about Monique. Jean refused my request for her protection. She's in danger and exposed, and it's a bit our fault."

"We'll take care of Monique ourselves," I said. "The plan for today—after breakfast, of course—is to go back and see Monique. We make sure she's okay, and I may have a few more questions for her. In her grief, she probably omitted some details that may wind up being important."

I started whipping up my version of the trucker's special for both of us.

"Hold the bacon on mine," Pat said. "Just keep it for Crackers. After breakfast, I need to go to my hotel to get a change of clothes and make myself presentable; then we go to Monique's."

"Okay, but you're already beyond presentable—you're edible."

Pat gave me a weak smile and said, "Saints protect me! The werebear is back."

I managed to snag a half a slice of French toast before Pat wolfed down the rest. Then shaved and showered while she did the dishes. I toweled off and zapped the bedroom television to the Weather Network. The consensus was that the weather gods were undecided. The forecast was for cool and windy, with a mixed bag: overcast morning, sunny breaks later, and potential evening showers.

When I walked into the living room, Pat was sitting in one of the overstuffed chairs, with Crackers on her lap. She was rubbing his neck and humming what sounded like an Irish lullaby.

"It's a bit cooler this morning, and the guy throwing darts at the weather chart is predicting evening showers," I said. "I don't know if we'll be in the house or staked out in the car. I've packed a duffel bag with an extra jacket, rainproof hunting vest, and a car blanket. Pack yourself a change kit when we get to your hotel. We don't know what will happen."

As I let Crackers out on the balcony, Pat headed for the coat-rack, slipped on her jacket, and reached into her pocket to check her phone log.

"Message from my lawyer. My gobshite ex-husband is up to more tricks, I'm sure."

As she listened to the message, her mouth opened and her eyebrows climbed up her forehead. I put my hand on her forearm as she thumbed the phone out of voice mail.

"Bad news?" I asked.

"To the contrary, Robert. The court battle is canceled. Mark has signed all the papers. He's contesting nothing. I get to keep my car, the house, and what little money was left in the joint bank account."

"Ye of little faith, I told you it would all work out," I said. "Mark is going to be too busy trying to keep his ass out of jail to bother your pretty butt anymore."

We stepped out into a bright, cool morning. The plan was simple: Pat would pick up some spare clothes, and then we would drop in on Monique. I was silently glad for Pat. With her ex finally out of the picture, I wondered what her future plans were. Would she move back to her house? I didn't dare ask; besides, I was enjoying her company and getting dangerously accustomed to having her at my apartment. Now's not the time to rock the boat, I told myself.

TWENTY-SEVEN

I was the designated driver again. Weekend traffic was predictably light. We hummed along in the fast lane, making it to Pat's hotel in record time. I was beginning to like the Wrangler. It was a solid car for a solid-size guy like me.

"You can come in if you want," Pat said. "I'm going to freshen up my makeup. Give me five minutes."

I opted for the fresh air and leaned against the hood of the Jeep. A minute later, Dobson called.

"Lieutenant, we found the victim's personal effects amongst George's pile of stuff behind the Dumpster. In her purse, we found the usual bag of makeup, and a wallet with no money, but her ID and credit cards were still in it. The killers may have searched her purse, then tossed it in the Dumpster. When we examined what was left of George this morning, he had a little over two hundred dollars on him. He may have seen the killers toss the purse and picked it up after the fact. It must have been in the Dumpster. It was pretty grungy—so bad, I couldn't get any good prints off it."

"Thanks, Dobson," I said. "I guess it'll be just another stray item in this case." I hung up after promising to keep him informed of my progress in the field. It was my way of keeping him hooked into the team. Other investigators used him for technical services but kept him out of the loop, so he often never knew how his efforts contributed to solving a case. I always figured it couldn't hurt to keep him interested.

Men are from Mars; women are from Venus. And on Venus, five minutes spent "freshening up" takes forty minutes. Still, when Pat came out the lobby door, it was worth the wait. She wore jeans as tight as the skin on a blueberry. She had taken my advice on warm, casual dress seriously. She was shod in hiking boots and had on a dark olive-green lumpy cashmere sweater. The lumps were all in the right places. She carried a leather overnight case with her jacket draped between the handles. I slid off my perch and opened the car door, and Pat tossed her bag into the rear seat.

"Nice bag," I said. "Looks expensive."

"Yes, pricey, but I fell in love with it. It was a present from me to myself. Every year, for my birthday I buy myself something special."

"I like the concept. I'm a month early for my birthday, but I think you're onto a good idea. I should do something special for me from me."

"Fair play to you," Pat said.

"By the way, when is your birthday?" I asked her.

"June twenty-ninth, but you'll never get the year out of me. A woman who can't keep her age a secret can't keep any secrets. Let's just say I'm old enough to know better but young enough to do it anyway."

"Ah, well, it's just a number." I said, "There's a Guatemalan proverb that says everyone is the age of their heart."

The banter continued as we headed to Monique Menard's house. As if to match the happy mood, the clouds were breaking up and the sun was peeking out. The road was clear and the motoring easy.

There was plenty of parking on the cross street below Menard's mansion, but I decided to swing up her street and down the next one just to check out the place first. A black Hummer was parked at a fire hydrant close to Menard's address.

"This looks like the car that followed us from the lake compound," I said.

"Robert, I've got me bad vibes again. We better check on Monique right now."

"Bang on, partner. Once is happenstance, twice is coincidence, and three times is enemy action."

We left the Jeep parked half on the sidewalk and partway into one of Menard's neighbors' driveway. I wedged my police card in a dashboard air vent.

Pat and I walked toward the house at a normal pace. I didn't want to bring attention to ourselves should someone be watching the outside of the building. As casually as possible, I looked up and down the street. I saw no one walking or loitering in the area. It didn't calm the bad vibes that I, too, was feeling. As we went up the pathway to Monique's front door, my policeman's mental radar was beeping, and I had butterflies flitting around in my gut.

Pat positioned herself across from me on the hinge side of the door. She lifted the right hem of her sweater, and her hand rested on her pistol butt. Without ringing the doorbell, I tried the door handle. It wasn't locked. With a slight groan, it swung easily into the foyer. The butterflies in my gut morphed into wheeling, diving condors. I pulled my weapon and clicked the safety off.

I motioned for Pat to stay a little behind me and to my left and watch my back.

We entered the vestibule with slow, careful, soundless steps. I kept myself and my pistol pointed straight ahead and, with my left hand open at my side, signaled Pat when to stop or move forward. Monique's house was eerily silent. As we crossed into the hallway, I glanced ahead at the wide stairs leading to the second floor. By peeking around the large newel post at the base of the stairs, I could see partway into the kitchen, at the rear of the house. No one was about. I motioned Pat to tack right, and we headed to the living room. I positioned myself beside the door frame, pivoted, and made a gun-first entry into the room. Pat maintained her position on the other side, watching and covering the area behind us. There was no one in this area, either. The house seemed deserted. I walked back to Pat and whispered, "There doesn't seem to be anyone around—give Monique a shout."

Pat backtracked to the wall at the bottom of the staircase and yelled up the stairs. "Monique, are you home? It's Patricia. I've brought you the cake recipe. Your front door was open."

I gave Pat a thumbs-up. But there was no response to her query.

My foot was on the bottom step, heading up, when I heard the unmistakable screech of a chair moving on a tile floor. I pointed to the kitchen and went around Pat, placing myself in front of her. We crept slowly down the hallway, hugging the right wall as we headed toward the kitchen. I held my gun at midlevel, with Pat following a yard behind me. We were eight or nine feet from the kitchen when a man dressed all in black, commando style, leaped from his hiding place on the right side of the room, to the center of the doorway. He was nearly as wide as I am and a foot taller. His face was covered with fine scars, like the loser on the barroom floor after a razor fight. He looked like a mean son of a bitch, and he was swinging an Uzi submachine gun up at me.

Electing to forgo the "Police, put your hands up!" formalities, I squeezed off two rounds so fast, it sounded like a single shot. I hit him square in the chest. He let out a grunt, turned slightly away from me, and staggered back a step but didn't go down. No blood was pouring from the holes my bullets had punched in his black multipocketed jacket. As he took the backward step, the Uzi stitched an arc of holes through the doorframe and along the corridor wall across from me.

At such close range, the gun blasts felt like a jackhammer banging away on my head. After the firing stopped, I could hear the ejected casings from the Uzi bouncing cymbal notes on the kitchen floor tiles. Flakes of drywall and shards of glass from a shattered picture frame had rained down onto me from the shot-up wall to my left.

All this happened in the space of about two seconds. Before he could get his balance, I charged toward him and fired two more shots at his big, ugly face. The first round hit him in the chin and exited through his right cheek just below the ear. The second shot punched through his throat, slicing his carotid artery on the way out. Blood sprayed rhythmically from the right side of his neck. He dropped to one knee but held on to the Uzi. At five feet, I fired another round, hitting him above the right eyebrow. He let out a moan and fell slowly backward from his knees, his feet tucked under his massive body.

For an instant, the world around me stopped. I felt frozen in time. My ears were ringing, and my nostrils stung from the acrid smell of burned gunpowder. Pumped with adrenaline, I registered everything as if it were happening in slow motion. I turned my head back around to check on Pat. She stood in the kitchen doorway behind me, her gun limp at her side, her face drained of color. She was looking blankly at the mess in front of me. The white kitchen tile contrasted with the bright-red spatter fanned out in a four-foot cone across the floor, the wide side to Pat's left and the small end pointing to the prone body. A pool of blood was spreading around the neck and head. A lump of brain matter oozed out of the back of his skull. In my mind, the event felt like a full-length movie, but only a few seconds had passed since we approached the kitchen.

Turning, I grabbed Pat by the arm and swung her back toward the front of the house, saying, "Don't look."

I was a bit late. She had already taken in the scene and was looking green around the gills, but otherwise unscathed.

"Are you okay?" I asked.

"I've seen worse after a bomb attack in Dublin. It was just that . . . for an instant, your man in the kitchen flashed me back to the blood and guts on the walls in Skipper's Alley. I'm okay now."

A thud resounded from upstairs. I grabbed Pat by the arm and dragged her behind me as we ran to the front of the house. As we approached the living room, I heard the sound of someone running along the second-floor hallway, toward us. A shadow appeared the top of the stairs. I feared it was another black-clad man in attack mode. We were in the open hallway, unprotected—in the kill zone for anyone firing from the head of the stairs. Still on the run, my full mass in movement, I pulled Pat from behind me and flung her into the living room as if she were no more than a bag of laundry. She rose off her feet and landed on her butt in one of the big armchairs. I had just made it to the living room entrance when Monique's sour-faced maid came bounding down the stairs. Her right hand slid along on the banister, and her skinny legs moved with the dexterity of a soccer forward. She bounced down the steps two at a time.

I yelled, "Monique?"

She screamed back, "In the safe room! He's behind me!"

Still in a run, she hit the floor and headed straight for the hall closet where, on our last visit, she had shown us the shotgun. Her pursuer slid into view at the top of the stairs. Before I could react, bullets ripped into the bottom steps and splintered the hardwood floor between the maid and me. I ducked into the living room, shifted the gun to my left hand, stuck my wrist around the doorframe, and let off three shots toward the top of the stairs. Pat was back on her feet, a yard behind me. She held her gun two-handed, pointed toward the ceiling. Dropping to my belly, I stuck my head out around the bottom of the door frame and stole a look up the stairs.

I recognized the hook-nosed, coffee-toting man from the compound. He still wore his black knit cap.

He was four or five steps down from the top of the stairs. My three shots had missed but had stopped him in his tracks. He was plastered face-first to the stairwell wall on the living room side. In his right hand, he held a MAC-10 automatic pistol fitted with a silencer. When I glanced up at him, he fired a short burst in my direction. The blup-blup of the suppressed gun echoed down the hall as the bullets shredded the hardwood molding inches from my head. Before I had the time to move, Pat aimed at the sound coming from his weapon. She fired five or six quick shots through the wall at him. Her bullets punched through the plaster and spun a picture frame off its hook, sending it cartwheeling down the stairs. One of her shots must have hit him in the arm or hand, because he dropped the machine pistol, and it tumbled down the stairs after the smashed painting.

Across the entrance hallway from me, the maid was crouched in the closet, with the door partly open. Through the narrow space, I saw that she held her shotgun bottom side up. She shoved shells into the loading slot as fast as a casino dealer flipping out the cards to a high-stakes player.

I heard my coffee man running through the second-floor corridor toward the back of the house. I was about to tell the maid that I was going after him when another black-clad man appeared in the front doorway. He was younger than the two others on his hit team. He was sallow skinned with shoulder-length, curly, dirty-blond hair. Left-handed, he pointed what looked like a Beretta 9mm at my head.

I dived back into the living room as he fired. As I fell, I felt the bullet tug my left sleeve. I landed hard on my butt, and the momentum slid me backward on the carpet. Without aiming, I raised my gun and fired two shots in his general direction. I couldn't tell whether I had hit him or not—only that it didn't faze him for a second. He continued toward me, wild-eyed as if he was on something scary. I rolled to one knee as he sent another bullet singing past my ear. Pat was crouched to my right and a bit behind me. She fired, hitting him high in the chest. He hesitated for a second as the panels in his bulletproof vest absorbed the impact.

He hadn't seen Monique's maid hiding in the closet behind him. His last step forward took him into her line of sight, and she let loose with the short Mossberg 12-gauge. In the enclosed area, it sounded like a howitzer. My ears started ringing again.

The buckshot ripped a strip from the side of his Kevlar vest at waist level. We were stuck in a cross-fire position, and some of the pellets fluffed up the rug at my side. He started turning rearward toward the maid as she jacked another shell into the chamber and pulled the trigger. Her second shot destroyed his knee. His whole body listed left, as if his remaining foot were rooted to the flooring. The maid was in my line of fire. I jumped to a better angle, took quick aim, and put a bullet through his right eye. He continued dropping to the floor like a felled tree. His head bounced on the hardwood floor, and everything went still.

My hearing returned, and I heard a moan from behind me. I whipped my head around. Pat was sitting on the floor, blood seeping from her jeans and spreading into the pale carpet beside her. She looked up at me and said in a weak voice, "Robert, my leg's shot off."

I bounded to Pat's side and yelled at the maid,

"How many left?"

She pumped another shell into the Mossberg and headed to the open front door. "There were three," she said. "I saw them from the upstairs bedroom as they were picking the lock to get in. I managed to get Monique into the safe room, and I hid in the bathroom. The third guy must have gone out from the back balcony and around to the front. He must have had enough. He just bugged off in a black Hummer."

"Never mind him," I said. "Get back here; I need help. Get me some towels or something."

The maid turned and headed to the kitchen, still carrying the shotgun. I tried to stop Pat's bleeding with my hands.

"You're going to be all right," I said. "It's a flesh wound. You picked up a couple of stray shotgun pellets. One of them must have nicked a vein. We just need compression on it."

Pat shivered. "It burns like the Divil's own fire, Robert. I don't like this. Don't like it at all, at all."

The maid returned with a stack of dish towels and a pair of scissors. She gave me a crooked smile. "You've made a real mess in my kitchen," she said. "Good work."

The maid slit Pat's painted-on jean leg from hem to hip, then cut off the fabric above the wound. She wiped the blood from above Pat's knee. There were a couple of small punctures in her thigh, and one bigger hole.

"Lucky," I said. "The pellets didn't hit anything serious. You don't need a tourniquet."

"Lucky, my pink-and-white arse! Real luck would have been not to get shot at all."

The maid folded a towel and handed it to Pat. "Press it to your leg and keep the pressure on it. I didn't realize you were behind. I didn't want to shoot you . . . I was aiming at him. It happened so fast. I'm so sorry."

"Not your fault. If I was a better markswoman, I'd'a put him down with my first bullet. This was my favorite pair of jeans, though."

I fished my phone out of my jacket pocket and was about to dial 911, then remembered my boss's warning concerning his niece's welfare.

"Pat, are you hanging on okay?" I said.

"Me leg's going some numb . . . I wouldn't dance a jig right now. But I'm all right, considering. Check on Monique if you want."

"Do your job here," the maid said. "I'll get Monique."

"Pat, I have a small problem about calling this in," I said.

"After all this, a small problem I can handle. What's the what, Robert?"

I gave her the summary version of Jean's final warnings to me. Then I said, "Monique's business belongs to the mob. I'm going to get them to help us out on this one."

"You play rough and loose, Robert, but I'll back up my partner all the way. In for a penny, and all that. Do what you have to, but it better include a doctor looking at my leg somewhere in there."

I called Antonio and left a message: "I'm at the Westmount place. We hit some contractor problems, and it's a bit of a mess. I need a cleanup crew and a doc for one of my team who had a small mishap with a nail gun."

I went around Pat and knelt at her back. I kept one hand pressed on the towel and wrapped my other hand around her shoulders so she could rest her head on my chest.

"You really know how to romance a girl," she said. "This was more craic than a New Year's party. Ah'm fair melted."

Five minutes later, Antonio and what looked like a tag team of four sumo wrestlers trooped in from the front door.

TWENTY-EIGHT

Antonio's crew made the bodies go away and had cleaned up most traces of the gunfight, even spackling the bullet holes and touching up the paint. The splintered baseboard and crown molding would have to wait a bit. I sat in one of the oversize chairs behind Pat, who was still on the floor and resting her back on my legs. Monique Menard sat on the other chair across from me.

Her maid, whose name was Marguerite but who was affectionately known by her employer as "Maggie," was busy cleaning up Monique's clothes. After releasing Monique from her bulletproof walk-in, Maggie had led her down the stairs. Monique took one look at the carnage at the bottom of her stairwell and barfed all over her thousand-dollar pj's.

I had given Antonio a summary of the shoot-out and told him about the gang's hideout up north.

"The spooks from CSIS and even the CIA want to poke their collective nose in," I said. "I'd prefer not to have them involved. If you can get a team together, I'd like to go pay them back for their visit here."

"Call me when you're ready," he said. "I missed all the action here, but I'm in on the next one."

"Let's meet at my place. I'll write down my address for you."

"Never mind. Just call me back with a time," he said. "I have your address, phone number, and the license of that new Jeep you're driving, in my phone."

Antonio knelt on the floor, working on patching Pat's leg.

"Is doctoring another one of your magic tricks?" I said. "That field dressing looks professional."

"Beaudry, in my line of work, patching yourself up is an essential skill. If you're going to do a job, you learn to do it right."

To Pat, he said, "I'm going to give you a card with an address for a private clinic. The doctor is a friend of mine. You have two, maybe three, pellets that have to be taken out. And you're going to need a tetanus shot."

"So I'm to be shot twice in the same day! Robert, I told you I had bad vibes."

Before I could comment, Pat turned to Monique. "You told us that Diana took pictures at the party with her phone. Did you take any with yours?"

"I took a few," she replied. "I suppose you want my phone."

Maggie, the badass maid, told me that the cell phone was in a charger in Monique's room. I understood her statement to mean go get it yourself. I found it on the night table in the frilly mirrored-ceilinged bedroom. I opened her "My Gallery" file. The first picture I scrolled to was one of the city councillor and my internal affairs nemesis, Detective Lorne Trehearne, both standing next to Hamid El-Rahim. This was not going to look good for Trehearn. I smiled. This was going to come in handy. I had just landed on the Monopoly "Get out of jail free" card.

TWENTY-NINE

But for the unmistakable hospital disinfectant smell, the private clinic could pass for a suite at the Hilton. Pat was sitting in a wheelchair, her left foot resting in a raised chrome-plated stirrup that projected from the front of the chair, the naked leg held straight out. A triage nurse in a crisp white uniform was examining the wound.

"You're going to need a tetanus shot," she said. "Have you gotten a tetanus vaccine in the last five years?"

"No," Pat replied, adding with a smirk, "I never planned on getting shot."

She packed more bandages on Pat's leg, asked for her blood type, and then took a blood sample from her finger anyhow.

I smiled at Pat. "O negative—who could guess? You're such a positive person."

The nurse checked Pat's vitals and then sent us to wait in the hall. After five or six minutes, she came back and put a bar coded plastic bracelet on Pat's wrist.

The nurse instructed us to go down the hall and wait in cubicle number 4. No longer in sight of hospital personnel, I dialed Antonio's number and left him a message to meet me at my apartment tomorrow morning.

Pat looked at me with eyes of ice.

"I really feel bad about you getting shot," I said. "I would have preferred taking it myself—easier to explain to your uncle, for one thing."

She wagged her finger at me. "It's none of that, you big oaf. You want to go up north to the compound with guns a-blazing. You're a chancer with a bleedin' capital 'C.' It'll catch up with you, Robert. If you don't get your eejit self kilt, sooner or later you'll have to answer to Uncle Jean and all the other agencies."

"Later is later," I said. "I don't want to talk to Jean or anybody else just yet. I'd rather give no more info than a half story in an envelope padded with question marks. We still don't know what they're doing up at the councillor's country house, nor who the hit teams are actually working for. I want to get to the bottom of this before I turn over anything."

"I don't like your Mr. Macho disregard for danger at all, at all," she said. Then she went silent and sullen, arms crossed in front of her.

I figured I'd do best not trying to win this discussion. I was skating on thin ice, and I knew it. "Talk to me about your time in Ireland," I said. "I've been to Paris and London but not Dublin. Always wanted to go to the land of forty shades of green."

The chill in Pat's eyes melted as she began regaling me with tales of her youth and the places she had been in Ireland.

Time and tides wait for no man, but when you're in a hospital, everybody waits for the doctor. About the time Pat had run out of stories, a kid straight out of internship came into our cubicle. He took her blood pressure, looked at the wounds, told her she needed a tetanus shot, scribbled some doctor gibberish on his notepad, and left. Fifteen or twenty minutes later, a middle-aged guy wearing jeans, a white coat, and a two-day beard came in.

Before he could open his mouth, I warned him, "Don't you dare tell us she needs a tetanus shot, and then leave like the other intern did."

He held up a little card but moved it too fast for me to read.

"I know about the tetanus shot. I'm just an orderly. I have to bring her up to surgery." He pointed to me. "You go back to the waiting room."

I did the badge-flip thing again. "She's involved in a murder case," I said. "I have to stay with her."

Pat glowered at me. "You bold bear! If I wasn't a capper, I'd give you me hobnails."

The orderly looked at me with question marks in his eyes. I shrugged my shoulders, and the three of us left the little cubicle.

After a short elevator ride and several twists and turns down identical-looking and -smelling corridors, he wheeled Pat into a narrow room with a long metal table in its center. A wall of glass-fronted cabinets filled with jars and boxes of medical supplies completed the stark decor. It looked like the same setup as for an autopsy. My cell phone rang, and the orderly shook his head at me and gave a "no-no" wag of his finger. I ignored him and answered the call.

Antonio was on the line. "Beaudry, what's your estimate on how many guys are at the compound up north?"

"Based on the number of ATVs, cars, and such, I figure six to eight, less the two from the raid on Monique's place."

"In that case, you and I will be enough—any more would be unsporting," Antonio said with a dry laugh.

"Pat would say that you're a chancer with a capital 'C.' But then, that's what she says about me, so welcome aboard."

"By the way," he said, "there are two guys staking out your house. Tomorrow, I'll come up from your back stairs."

"Okay, I know who they are," I said. "I have to cut you short—Pat's going into surgery and they don't allow cell phones in here. I'll call you back."

I hung up and slid my phone back into my pocket as a surgeon in green scrubs came in. He gave me a dirty look. I did the badge-flip thing once more. A couple more days like this, and I'd give myself carpal tunnel syndrome.

The doctor had the bedside manner of a cape buffalo, and the same smile as Monique's maid, Maggie, which is to say, none. In a clipped tone, he shot orders right and left. "Where's the table pad? Get a table pad. Call the duty nurse."

He took the little card from the orderly and spoke as if we weren't there. "Did anybody do an X-ray? Where are the X-rays? Did she get a tetanus shot?"

"No, I didn't get a shot," Pat said. "But a drop of Bushmills Malt would do just fine in the meantime."

He undid her bandage, looked at the punctures, and gave me a tight smile. "Oh, she's going to need a bit more than whiskey for this. We're going to have to dig those out."

He sent Pat and her chauffeur a couple of rooms down the hallway for X-rays. A few minutes later, they wheeled back in. Pat carried a folder with her X-rays on her lap.

The doctor got the nurse to organize the room and paint Pat's thigh with some orange gloop. While the surgeon was setting up and grumbling, the nurse gave Pat the tetanus shot, followed by something else, which made her go cross-eyed and limp.

They lifted her onto the table. The doctor poked here and there with a little syringe of Xylocaine to numb the wounds. Pat dozed off and on while the surgeon did his job.

The room was narrow, and I wasn't. I stood in a corner, doing my best to stay out of the operating team's way. An hour and a quarter later and with aching feet, I followed Pat as the orderly wheeled her to another room to wait for a prescription the doctor had written out. The drugs had downshifted her to sleepy-turtle mode.

"Are you gonna drive me to my hotel?" she said. "I wanna go to sleep. My arms and head are too heavy."

The nurse came in with the antibiotics and some painkillers, then motioned me over to her desk, where I signed a half ream of papers.

"She was lucky to get Doctor Dahan today," she said. "He's a marvel. He did a lateral ligature on the LSV, and his exterior sutures are so fine, she won't even have a scar."

"Well, that's a shame. If you get shot and survive, you should at least have a memento of the event."

The nurse looked me up and down. "That's fine for a big, handsome brute like you, but I don't think your girlfriend would appreciate scars during swimsuit season."

"Sergeant O'Neil is not my girlfriend; she's my partner. And I don't speak Doctorese, so I haven't a clue what an LSV is."

"Well, you two looked like a couple, and Doctor Dahan did a great job. Just make sure she doesn't walk around until tomorrow, or it may start bleeding again. Also, she'll be drowsy for the next three to four hours. Let her sleep it off."

She got up, sat on the corner of her desk, and crossed her legs. "So you're single . . ."

"Freshly divorced and widowed."

She gave me a cute sideways grin—alluring, but nowhere close to Pat's titanium-melting power smile. She handed me a sheet from a prescription pad. "My number's on the back—just in case you need, um, anything."

I gave her a smile and a wink and went back to Pat, who was trying to move her wheelchair forward with one of the brakes still engaged.

"Piece of crap, this thing drives like me Uncle Seamus after a night at the Temple Bar."

"I'll push you around, Pat," I said. "I don't want to leave you alone. I'll take care of you at my place."

"S'o-o-kay," she said.

She stopped struggling with the wheelchair and let me drive. As I rolled her to the exit, she had her eyes closed, and a little smile on her face.

THIRTY

I carried Pat up the stairs to my apartment. She was zonked from the anesthesia and couldn't navigate on her own. Picking her up was no problem—she weighed barely over 130 pounds, shoes and all. I could bench-press twice that with a bad flu and a hangover. The challenge was my width plus the length of her legs, which were sticking out from over my right forearm. And what spectacular legs they were! I had to go up sideways, one stair at a time.

As I tried to hold on to her and unlock my front door at the same time, my second-floor tenant came up the stairs. Helping me open the door, he said in a sarcastic tone, "This is the second time I see you bring a doped-up woman to your apartment, Robert. If you weren't a cop, I'd have to call one."

"First of all," I said, dipping my shoulder so her feet would clear the doorjamb, "note the heavily bandaged leg. My police partner was shot in an incident today. She just got out of surgery. And second, you're just jealous."

At the top landing, Pat looked down the hallway behind me and giggled softly. I turned to see Crackers's handiwork: four little piles of shredded toilet paper, equally spaced along the center of the corridor. It looked like the white lines down the center of a highway.

"Not again. I'm sure there's some all over the house."

Pat punctuated her giggling with hiccups. I had to find out what the doctor had given her—it was even stronger than the little tube drinks from Pink's. She was feeling no pain and having a grand old time. I set her gently down into one of the overstuffed living-room chairs. Her head tilted to one side as she sank into the cushions.

"Mmmmm," she said.

I dropped my jacket onto a kitchen chair, then put the cell phone and gun on the kitchen counter. The sound woke Crackers, who, for some unknown reason, was sleeping in the geographic center of the breakfast table. He jumped down and followed me back to the living room.

He came up to Pat, caught one whiff of hospital smell, and took off like a member of Parliament escaping a bordello raid.

I touched Pat on the shoulder. "Do you want me to make you a cup of tea, or do you just want to go to sleep?"

"Nnmmm," she replied.

I interpreted this that as opting for the latter. Not only was she still half sedated, but also, Pat was not used to gunplay. The reaction to a fight-or-flight situation is to flood the body with adrenaline to meet the immediate danger, and as the body powers down after the stressful event, the person will frequently nod off to sleep.

I cleaned up my bedroom, turned down the sheets, fluffed up the pillows, and went back to the living room to carry Pat back to my room.

She sat on the edge of my bed, wobbly as a five-month-old baby.

"I took off your shoes," I said. "I'll have to take off what's left of your jeans."

Pat opened her eyes. "Are you trying to take advantage of me now?"

"No, your pants are a bloody mess, and those are two-hundred-thread-count sheets."

"Ah, ye jibber. Always a gentleman." Pat started giggling again.

A minute later, she was under the sheets, eyes shut and a big grin on her kisser.

My cell phone rang from the kitchen counter. I managed to catch the call before the last ring. Captain O'Neil assailed my ear.

"What happened with CSIS? Beaudry, when I say call me back, I mean as soon as you know, not a week later."

"It's not a week later; it was last night," I said. "Two guys, supposedly from the American embassy, called on me sometime around eleven. They showed me the picture of the buffet table that Dobson printed from Diana's phone. Standing behind the ice sculpture are a Swiss banker and a known terrorist. He's number six on their most-wanted list. That's what all the fuss is about. I have no news from the RCMP or CSIS. They probably have their politically correct heads in the sand, pretending nothing is going on. I think some arm of the CIA has unofficially taken over. I have my suspicions that the spooks will let out the word that Monique has the pictures, and use her as bait to draw in the terrorist crew. Since you've refused protection for Monique, Pat and I decided to check up on her. We're staking out her place now. I was just about to call you to report in."

"Bob Beaudry, you shovel it like an organic gardener in springtime."

I ignored him and continued with my story. "Pat and I will stay on stakeout here to protect Monique, but maybe we should let the spooks do their thing. If something goes down, good or bad, let them take the credit or the crap, and we can keep the spooks, the jihadis, and the councillor out of the story. We can always use poor crazy, dead George as a scapegoat and pin Monique's case on him. He did have her purse in his stuff, and he did take her money. We'd come out of the mess with a closed case and smelling like a rose."

I could just see Jean on the other end of the line, worrying his upper lip, his little mustache wiggling like a nervous caterpillar under his nose.

"I'm not totally at ease with that, but I must admit, you shovel it exceedingly well, Beaudry. No one's going to believe the spies-and-terrorists story anyhow. The RCMP, CSIS, and the Americans won't hassle us, and it simplifies the paperwork. I'll think about it. Call me back if anything happens at your stakeout. I want the case closed in the next forty-eight hours, one way or the other."

"You're the boss," I said.

Before he hung up, Jean said, "When it comes to you, I'm never quite certain of that."

My feline fiend came into the room, his fur all tangled and a dust bunny hitchhiking on the base of his tail.

"You've been hiding under the dresser again, haven't you," I said.

Pat walked into the kitchen, and Crackers took off again.

"You're not supposed to be walking around, Pat. Just call me if you need anything."

"I need a glass of water," she said. "I'm as parched as a salmon in a sand pit."

I sat her down and poured her a glass, and she drank it slowly while I told her about my conversation with her uncle.

"Pinning a murder on poor homeless George—you should be ashamed of yourself, Robert! I'd expect better from you."

"Diana found love and had inherited a large chunk of money," I said. "She was where we'd all like to be in life. I'm sure she and her girlfriend Monique had dreams they wanted to realize. They had a chance, and a right, to be happy. Those animals took it all from them, and they'll never see a day in jail if we rely solely on the courts and do everything by the book. Our legal system doesn't always deliver justice. I can't count how many criminals I've caught who got off scot-free due to some bullshit technicality."

"I'd feel bad about framing your poor man George," Pat said. "But for them that done Monique in, it's a crime that should not go unpunished. Ah'm agreed to that, but it doesn't mean that you don a red cape and go dashing off to take on the villains all by yourself now."

"The terrorists will bargain freedom for some information the spy agencies want, and that'll be the end of the story," I said. "I can't sleep well with that. I'd prefer dishing out a bit of justice on my own—sans red cape, of course. For that to happen, I need a favor from George. Now I owe him one."

I picked up my cell phone, put it on speaker, and dialed.

"Hi, this is Lieutenant Bob Beaudry," I said to the lady who answered the phone. "Is Father Pierce around? I'd like to speak with him if at all possible."

Seconds later, Alex Pierce came on the line. “Hi, Robert. What warrants this late call? Nothing wrong, I hope.”

“No, not today, Alex. I just need a small favor. There’s a homeless person in the morgue. His name is George Banks. I need you to arrange a decent burial for him. I’ll take care of the financial end.”

Father Pierce hung up after his usual admonitions and warnings about my getting too personally involved in my work.

“You’ve partially redeemed yourself now, you have,” Pat said “The charm of you is that you’re a romantic who acts a modern version of a knight in shining armor. But I’m not sure your philosophy of justice is going to get those broad shoulders through the Pearly Gates. Yourself may wind up with the armor a bit tarnished.”

I knelt in front of Pat and hefted her up. With a nonchalant smile, I said, “Everything has a cost. A bit of rust is the least of my worries.”

She took my hand. “Bring me back to bed, ya silly bear.”

THIRTY-ONE

I woke to the sound of Crackers pushing his food bowl around on the kitchen tiles. It took me a few seconds to register my surroundings. I was spooned behind Pat, my left arm around her, and my hand under her right breast. I knew that she had fallen asleep as soon as I cuddled her in bed and that nothing had happened. I was still fully dressed. I slid my arm out and rolled gently off my side of the bed. The bedside clock's soft green numerals read"6:06." I was late with Crackers's breakfast.

When I stepped into the kitchen, my temperamental roomie was nowhere to be seen. I rattled his food plate, to no avail.

"Okay, how about a nice can of Cat and Kitten Turkey Feast with added antioxidant vitamins?" I coaxed.

The whirr of the can opener enticed him from his hideaway. A tangle of black and white fur, trimmed with dust, popped out from the space between the side of the refrigerator and the kitchen counter.

I fed him and made a mental note to give him a good brushing later, when I had time and energy enough for that battle. I had a bigger fight to plan for, but first I needed something to eat. I was starving. I was feeling aches and pains in muscles that I didn't even know I had, and my mouth had a bitter, metallic taste. Strange how coming through a life-and-death situation makes you hungry. I poured myself a large bowl of granola and topped it with two handfuls of blueberries. I ate and then I made Pat's usual French toast topped with fruit and maple syrup.

"I don't understand how she can eat like a lumberjack and stay so trim," I said to Crackers. He sniffed the air and took off to hide once more in the six-inch gap between the counter cabinets and the refrigerator.

"I do not eat like a lumberjack," Pat said from behind me.

"I stand corrected," I said. "You eat like a lumberjill, and you even look the part when you're in my blue checkered Orvis shirt."

At the moment, she was wearing her green cashmere sweater, pink panties, and a wide bandage six inches above her left knee.

I pointed at her. "That looks good, too. The garter is a bit simple, but it helps you pull off that cute dissolute-wench look."

"I couldn't find my soft blue shirt," Pat said.

"Your blue shirt is at the dry cleaner. Its green sibling is in the spare-bedroom closet. And if you insist on walking around the house dressed like that, I may be tempted to have you for breakfast dessert." I threw in an exaggerated leer."

"Hah! Idle threats—I'm sure now. I need some cling wrap to protect my bandage. I'll shower, then have breakfast after. Is that okay, Mr. Werebear?"

I handed her the plastic wrap and gave her a wolf whistle as she headed back down the hall.

An hour later, my tai chi routine was done and we were back at the breakfast table. From her overnight kit, Pat put on a tweedy light-gray vest over a simple white T-shirt. A matching gray pencil skirt completed the look.

"I'm probably biased," I said, "but you manage to look good in anything you put on."

"'At's one of my many talents. When I wasn't tied down to a computer, I took part in some of our fraud investigations. I used to go undercover as a tax auditor, a businesswoman, or an IT expert. I learned to dress the part. As much as I didn't like the desk part of the job, I really liked the investigative side. We would set up sting operations and trap con men and other swindlers who were defrauding rich old ladies of their savings. We went after all kinds of gougers, from bank embezzlers to big multilevel marketing companies."

Looking down, she shook her head slowly. "That's where I met Mark. He was representing an industrialist we were investigating. Mark was elegant and smooth-talking in defending the guy."

"Well, you're dressed very businesslike today," I said. "Though I still prefer the pink panties and bandage-garter look."

"Robert, if you can be serious for a moment, I need your help today. I got a text from my lawyer when I was in the shower. I have to meet her this morning at my old house. I need to accept the condition of the property and sign off on a bunch of other documents. Apparently, she has to present everything in court first thing Monday morning, or else the investigators at Revenue Québec may include my stuff in Mark's assets and seize everything. I'd spend months in court trying to get back what's mine."

"My plan to get your crazy ex to stop harassing you may have backfired," I said. "I have to make it right. You can count on me for anything you need."

"I'll text her back to confirm a meeting in an hour at the house," Pat said.

"I'll drive," I replied.

I was glad to help her. It was my gunplay karma that had got her wounded, and now I was involving her as an accomplice before the fact in my iffy plan to go after the terrorists who had killed Diana. And yet, she didn't complain or even think of reporting to her uncle about my disregard for official rules. Pat was a class act. I owed her big time.

THIRTY-TWO

The house where Pat and her ex-husband had lived was in the West Island suburbs. On this bright, balmy morning, the whole world seemed to be out for a Sunday drive. From my condo downtown, the fifteen-minute hop took us forty-five minutes. After several zigs and meanders around mazelike crescents and semicircular lanes, I backed the Jeep into her driveway.

"Do I get rally points for finding the house?" I said. "This part of town is a navigator's nightmare."

"I never liked the location. Mark got it at a bargain price from a client of his who was getting a divorce. He made some underhanded cash deal with the guy to lowball the official selling price so the ex-wife would get less money in the settlement."

"That should have given you a hint about Mark's true colors." I said.

"Green is 'envy'; red is 'anger.' I dunno what color 'cheating gobshite' is. I only found out about his slimy deal on the house after we moved in. In fact, I didn't want the suburban life at all, at all. You need to drive out of the development for everything. No such thing as a leisurely stroll to the local pub around here. In Dublin, everything was within walking distance. I loved that."

"Well, we're here now," I said. "Are you going to give me the grand tour?"

We got out, and Pat showed me around the property. The lawn and hedges looked pretty sad. The place was going back to wild. I knew that Pat was a city girl, and I could see that her ex was not much of a gardener. It was a shame, because they had a double-large property with an in-ground pool and some nice mature trees that stood straight and proud all around the bungalow. Situated in an older part of the suburbs, the house must have been built some twenty-odd years ago. Uncared for, it was starting to look its age.

"The house is part of the divorce deal," Pat said. "But I don't want the bloody place. I couldn't live here anymore. I'd never feel at home, and there are too many bad memories. It'll be up for sale as soon as I can manage it."

"If I can put in my two cents' worth of unsolicited advice, you should spend a few dollars freshening up the place before you list it. Good staging really makes a difference in the selling price. If you need help, I'll volunteer. I'm a good handyman. I did most of the renovations on my condo myself."

"I may take you up on that. The house looks as shoddy as Mark's ethics."

The negotiations on my offer of help were cut short by the arrival of a new-looking black Porsche Cayenne and a dirty-red Ford F-250 pickup. Pat's lawyer had come with someone else in tow.

Her attorney was a good-looking thirty-something short-haired brunette who dressed ten years too young for her age. The tight, short skirt and matching jean jacket didn't jibe with the wrinkles around her eyes and neck, which her makeup tried valiantly to hide.

She made up for her what-not-to-wear wardrobe with a professional take-charge attitude.

"Good morning, Pat. I brought along Mr. Grimaldi, from GRM House Inspection Services. I want everything checked out before I let you sign on the dotted line."

Pat's pert lawyer gave me a more-than-pert smile. "Who's your hunky bodyguard, Pat?"

Pat did the introductions, and we shook hands all around. I volunteered to take notes and help Grimaldi, the house inspector, unload his ladder and do the survey. Pat and Susan, the lawyer, went into the house to review legal affidavits and contract documents.

The inspection and legalese took a little under two hours. The house had been built in the days when contractors took pride in their work, and construction standards were not corrupted by the appeal of a fast dollar. Pat's house didn't have structural issues. With the exception of a collapsed driveway drain, the needed repairs were all simple cosmetics.

Mr. Grimaldi gave his report to Susan, Pat signed here and initialed there, all in triplicate, and Mr. Grimaldi and Susan departed.

"Robert, I can't breathe in this house," Pat said. "I just want to get rid of it now and start my life over. I want to pack some more clothes and personal stuff. It'll take me a few minutes, if you don't mind waiting."

"Just do what you need to," I said. "You've signed all the legal stuff, and now you're free to be in charge of your destiny."

"I've always been in charge of my life," she said. "Even with Mark's bullying and shenanigans, I never surrendered an inch of me. It was just a constant, tiring battle. I feel like a ten-ton weight's been lifted off my back."

Pat went to do her packing. I knew that her few minutes were going to be in Venus time, I did the math, and figured I had plenty of time to channel surf her big-screen TV in the living room.

Twenty-five minutes of Discovery Channel later, I was an expert on cuttlefish and their ability to change color as protection or to hypnotize their prey. My education on the multitentacled little mollusc's life and habits was interrupted by Pat's phone, vibrating its way toward the edge of the glass coffee table in front of me.

"Pat, your phone is trying to jump off of the coffee table," I yelled. "Want me to answer?"

"Okay, but it may be Uncle Jean, so careful of what you say."

"Good morning," I answered. "James the butler speaking."

"What? Who is this?"

"Lieutenant Beaudry. This is Pat O'Neil's line."

"Beaudry, this is Commissioner Martin—Bernard Martin. I had heard you were a smart aleck. I see that it's true. I need to speak to Patricia, and you need to practice your British accent. Your James-the-butler imitation was pathetic."

"Okay, Commissioner, I stand chastened," I said. "I'll pass you to Pat."

I brought Pat her phone and went back to my channel surfing. A minute or so later, she came into the living room.

"That was a strange call," she said. "The boss of my ex-boss wants urgently to see me."

"What's that all about?" I said. "Are you in trouble? That's supposed to be my area."

"'At's a fact. Indeed, the commissioner did ask me if you had got me in trouble. I told him not yet, but there was always hope." Pat had a soft smile on her lips, and a bedroom look in her eyes that made me want to ravish her then and there.

I had to swallow a couple of times before I could speak.

"So he called you to ask if I got you in trouble?" I croaked.

"No, silly, he wants to meet me at headquarters at six thirty tomorrow morning. He said it was a top-secret meeting and that he couldn't tell me anything more over the phone."

Before I could comment, her phone buzzed again. She took the call, which lasted maybe ten seconds.

"Another cloak-and-dagger call?" I asked.

"No, your friends from the shady car repair place just told me my car is like new and is parked in front of your house. Thank you again, Robert."

Pat stepped in close, got up on her tiptoes, and put her arms around my neck and kissed me gently on the cheek. I put my arms around her and held her, but I said, "We better get out of here and back to police business before we really do get in trouble. It's not the place or the time."

She dropped her arms from my neck, but I pressed her to me for a couple of seconds before letting go.

"You're right, Werebear," she said as she turned away from me.

We packed the Jeep with her suitcases, boxes, and bags and headed back to Old Montreal.

THIRTY-THREE

I parked the Jeep three cars behind Pat's Mustang. Nico's cousin and his Midnight Auto Parts and Repair crew had done a superb job. The silver flakes in the paint shone as if backlit.

"I think they gave you the intensive polishing packaging as well as the hood repair," I said.

"You're not slagging—it looks better than new," Pat said with a grin as wide as Bernie's waistline. "Do you want to bring the Jeep back to the shop? I can follow you and drive you back."

"No need. I've decided to take your advice and get myself a birthday present from me to me. I'm going to keep the Wrangler. I'll call Nico's cousin tomorrow and work out a deal."

"Fair play. The car is big and strong, like you. It suits you. Congratulations." Pat put her hand out, and we shook. It gave me a bothered feeling. After the long hug at her house, shaking hands felt like getting the cold shoulder. I hoped I hadn't offended her when I said we had to get back to police business. Although I had promised myself to keep everything on a strictly professional level, I could no longer ignore that I had fallen ass over teakettle for this woman. This was not a good situation. Not only was it against department policy, but I wasn't certain how my feelings for her would be reciprocated. I had about the same odds of understanding a woman's thought process and interpreting what she was saying as I had of solving the Riemann hypothesis.

Luckily for me, before I could say something that would get me in trouble, Pat said, "I have to get up early tomorrow morning for an important meeting at headquarters. Since most of my clothes are still at my hotel, I'm going to pick up the overnight bag I left here, and the bags in your new Jeep, and head to my hotel."

I said, "I can go upstairs and get your bag for you. You shouldn't overstress your leg."

"Ah, not a bother; the leg is fine. Apart from nicking a vein, the pellets were just like a splinter in the flesh—they lost most of their clout bouncing off the carpet and floor. In any case," she added with a grin, "the Irish ignore anything they can't drink or punch."

We went up the stairs, and I was still wondering if something had gone astray.

Pat headed to the bedroom to get her stuff, and I headed to the bathroom. I slid my house key into a slot on the side of the big framed mirror over the sink. The tapered end of the key pushed up a lock pin, and the mirror swung open to reveal a smaller steel panel in the wall. I pressed the code on the miniature keypad in its center.

The teardown renovations I had done over the past half year gave me the chance to add a few enhancements to the house. This secret gun vault was one of them. I put my service weapon away and pulled out a pair of CZ-85 combat pistols, along with two spare sixteen-round magazines. From the bottom shelf, I grabbed a hundred-round box of Winchester 9mm Luger shells. I closed the wall safe, piled my gear in the crook of my arm, and headed to the kitchen.

I could hear Crackers growling in the hallway. From experience, I recognized his warning that a stranger was in the house. I peeked into the kitchen. Antonio was sitting at the table. He had an extra-large duffel bag at his feet and was engaged in a staring contest with Crackers, who had his hackles up and was giving a fair imitation of a panther's throaty growl. I sat down on a chair opposite Antonio as Crackers dashed out toward the bedroom.

"How'd you get in?" I asked. "The doors were locked."

"If you have the right tools, any lock can be bumped—even your front door's fancy Mul-T-Lock."

"I'm sure the average burglar doesn't have your skill set," I said. "I'll take my chances."

In another fast move, Antonio snatched one of the pistols from me and laid it gently on the table, extracting the magazine as he did so.

"I approve of your choice of weapons, Beaudry," he said as he fieldstripped it.

Before I could answer, Pat came into the kitchen. She dropped her bag on the floor when she saw Antonio.

"How's the leg, Sergeant?" he asked.

"Just a scratch," she said, eyeing all the hardware. "Thanks for the field dressing. What's all the artillery for?"

"Just admiring your partner's choice of tools," Antonio said. "Well maintained, but maybe a little too much gun oil. It'll gum up the ejector and can stovepipe a round."

"Stovepipe?" Pat said.

Antonio pulled the weapon's slide back and stuck his index finger in the breech, imitating a jam. "The gun fires, but the empty casing doesn't eject properly—jams vertically in the ejection port, like a little stovepipe sticking out."

"Your technical discourse doesn't answer my first question, though, does it, now?"

"We're just trading war stories, Pat," I said.

"Blarney if I ever heard it. You boys are up to mischief, a'm sure of it. I'll be off now before you get me involved in your scheming."

I got up to say good-bye to Pat, but she turned away and said, "Robert, I'll call you tomorrow with news of my meeting with the commissioner."

As she closed the front door, Antonio said, "You sweethearts have a little tiff? Your girlfriend looked a bit uptight."

"She's my partner, not my girlfriend."

Antonio looked at me with his head down, as if peering over a pair of glasses.

"I read how you both look at each other." He pulled out his wallet and slipped a hundred-dollar bill under the edge of my placemat. "I'll bet you two to one you're in bed with her before the month is out."

"You're gonna lose your money, Antonio. It's against department policy. I just got off a suspension, and I'm not itching for another one."

"Speaking of your vulnerable areas," Antonio said, "I brought you a present." From his overstuffed duffel, he pulled out a white mesh undershirt with Kevlar panels covering the front and back. "We're not going into battle without you in proper dress."

"Okay, Daddy, no arguments here," I said. "I saw part of their arsenal."

Antonio reached into his duffel. "We've got our own goodies."

He pulled out two Browning Hi Power pistols, a silenced Colt Woodsman, a tactical semiautomatic shotgun, two tear-gas grenades, and two pairs of military-grade night goggles.

"Never mind Pat—I think I've just fallen in love with you," I said, with my hand over my heart.

We ordered pizza, ate, and reviewed my notes and the pictures of the compound that I had taken with my phone. And over the next two hours, we formulated a plan of attack. We decided to follow the same trail I had used on my previous visit and to hit the camp just before dawn. We would enter from the river side, which would ensure that the enemy was in front of our line of fire and that no one was behind us.

"Our weapons are all in order, so we can get a few hours' sleep," I said. "I'll set an alarm on my phone."

"No need—I'll wake you in time," Antonio said as he sank into one of the overstuffed living-room couches. He started snoring at the end of his sentence, as if he had turned off a switch.

THIRTY-FOUR

I snapped awake when Antonio tapped me on the head.

"Come on, Beaudry, shake a leg. I made us some sandwiches for the trip while you were still in dreamland."

Not to be outdone, I bounded out of my chair and slipped on the Kevlar vest in the same motion. I scooped up the rest of the weapons and equipment that I had left at my feet, grabbed my leather jacket, and said, "Let's get to it."

Antonio smiled as he slipped on a double holster over his bulletproof vest. He zipped up his hooded windbreaker and picked up the duffel bag, and we headed to the door.

We had decided to take the Jeep. Antonio tossed our supplies on the backseat and crossed the street to open the trunk of a black Mercedes. He pulled out what appeared to be a large pile of leaves and twigs and dumped the mess next to his duffel.

"What the heck is that for?" I asked.

"Invisibility cloaks of sorts. It's two Ghillie suits. That should blend us into the scenery."

"I really think I am in love," I said. "You think of everything."

"Not really. I haven't come up with a plan B yet. Beaudry, you got the map coordinates for the country place?"

"Yup, pinned it on my GPS app. Here's my phone."

Antonio opened the app, then used my phone to call someone. I heard only his end of the conversation, but it was clear to me that he was planning for any eventuality.

"Vic, I just texted you some coordinates. If I don't call you back by ten this morning, I want you to set a chopper down as close as possible to that spot. Make sure you have an emergency med kit on board, and bring along Mickey and his long gun."

He hung up and handed me my phone. I said, "You're planning a fast exit. This doesn't bode well for our friendship."

"I told you, always have a plan B. If anything goes wrong for either of us, head back to the woods and wait for the chopper. Don't be a hero—get your ass out of there."

"We started this together and we'll end it together, Antonio."

"Beaudry, from what I hear, you're a good cop. Why the hell are doing this?"

"Because I'm a good cop. We're dealing with terrorists, a crooked foreign banker, and slimy politicians. They've killed innocent people on my watch, and I know from experience that unless we deal out the justice ourselves, they'll never see a day in jail. Everything will be swept under a very large rug."

He shook his head. "I understand your frustration with the system, but you're doing something wrong to do something right."

"I could ask you the same question," I said. "Your boss said to help me if you could. I'm pretty sure he didn't have this level of backup in mind."

Antonio tugged his hood down and smoothed it around his back collar, then turned to face me as I buckled my seat belt.

"Beaudry, I became a criminal not because I was born a bad person but because, somewhere along my road, I had to choose this career or death. I decided to live and to become the best at what I had to do. I have my own values, which are wider than the law allows, and I never have to explain or apologize for my actions. Besides, I can use your justification: your terrorists tried to kill two of my people on my watch."

"Okay, I'm hoist by my own petard," I said. "I never thought you were a bad guy, just a good criminal. Some French poet wrote, 'There is no man so good that if he placed all his actions and thoughts under the scrutiny of the laws, he would not deserve hanging ten times in his life.' I guess we both fit that description."

Antonio double tapped on the shifter. "Hey, I got a great idea: how about you shut up and drive before I change my mind on backing you up."

"Okay," I said. "We stick with the plan."

We headed north and reached the village turnoff in record time. Now that I knew where I was going, the road felt a lot shorter than the first time.

Before we got too deep into the woods, Antonio told me to pull over. He got out, opened the door on my side, fiddled under the dashboard, and pulled out the fuse for the headlights. "From here on, we use the night goggles."

His equipment was state of the art. It gave a pale-green glow to everything, but otherwise, the road was as clear as day. I could have dodged a baby rabbit in the road. We went up the same path that Pat and I took earlier, and parked on the logging road but without backing the Jeep into the underbrush.

I took the shotgun, and Antonio took the silenced Colt and the grenades. He unfolded the camouflage suits. The Ghillie was more of a cloak that went over our heads than a suit. I was five feet from him, and as soon as he put it on, I could hardly distinguish the shape of a man.

We stepped into the underbrush. I easily found the trail marker that I left on my last trip. It hadn't rained in the past few days, and my little pyramid was still standing. With the goggles and our camo wraps, we made slow time down the trail to the lake. An hour later, we were crouched by the boathouse and the big power generator.

Antonio raised his fist head high, indicating that I should freeze in place. With two fingers, he pointed to where his eyes would be if he weren't a walking thicket of ferns and moss. Then he pointed toward the hut on our right and made a circular motion with his hand, indicating that he was going to scout the area.

According to our plan, I was to wait five minutes, then switch off the generator.

A few minutes after Antonio had blended into the scenery, an armed man came walking from around the side of the hut Antonio had headed for. The night goggles didn't give me colors, just varying shades of green, but the man appeared to be wearing jeans and a light-colored jacket. I was expecting only the black-clad men I had seen on my first visit. I hoped this didn't mean there were now more recruits in the camp.

The man carried his weapon slung leisurely over his right shoulder, the barrel pointed toward the ground. He walked to the front of hut, and just as he was about to reach for the door handle, Antonio pulled another of his unexpected fast moves. He jumped out from the darkness, flipped off his Ghillie suit, and, in the same motion, hugged the man from behind. The man slumped, and Antonio backed up and gently laid him down at the side of the door. I never saw a weapon or heard a sound.

Antonio moved to the door and tried to open it. There must have been an infrared camera or a motion sensor around it, because lights turned on around the hut and camp perimeter, and I could hear an alarm beeping from inside the main building. My goggles reacted to the glare and dimmed out. I flipped them off and hit the kill switch on the generator as Antonio ducked back into the woods. Most of the lights went off, but some were on a battery backup and remained lit. I heard the snap-snap of Antonio's silenced .22 as the light over the hut's door shattered and blinked out.

I grabbed the twelve-gauge and headed toward the main house. I was ten feet from the side door when it opened. The hook-nosed guy from my first visit stared straight at me, his submachine gun pointed at me but low. I was still clad in the Ghillie suit, so he wasn't sure what he was looking at. He hesitated for a tenth of a second too long. I fired first. The buckshot hit him in the neck and face and pushed him back against another man, who was walking out behind him. I chambered another shell and pulled the trigger. The second man staggered but responded with a pistol shot that went way over my head. He ducked back into the house as I ran forward, firing at his disappearing shadow. Sensing that he was waiting for me, I dropped to one knee and leveled the shotgun as I entered into the main hallway. From a partly opened door at the end of the hall, he poked out his head and arm and fired two shots in my direction. I was in darkness, and with no horizon to judge my position by, he shot high again. Unfortunately for him, the light coming from the room behind dimly backlit him, and the muzzle flash from his gun gave away his exact position. I didn't give him a second chance. Knowing that he probably wore a ballistic vest, I shot at his legs, then, as he twisted, shot him in the face.

I shrugged off my Ghillie suit and crept forward. The terrorist had fallen half in and half out of the doorway. In the room, someone was speaking on a two-way radio. I could hear the crackle when the other party answered, and the sound of gunfire in the background. I was certain that Antonio was wreaking havoc outside. I left the shotgun on the floor, changed to my 9mm pistol, and fired six shots rapidly through the door, toward the sound of the voice.

Staying low, I moved to the door opening. The wall in front of me was covered with flat screens and radio equipment. On my left, the bald guy I had seen in the black Humvee on my first visit was bleeding from an arm wound and reaching for the pistol he had dropped when my bullet struck him. I came at him, firing.

My barrage ended his reach and shattered two of the monitor screens, raining shards of glass and plastic over him as he dropped to the floor. I looked down at him.

"Greetings from Diana, the woman you shot in the parking lot," I said. "What goes around, and all that."

He looked up at me, wide eyed, for a second, then coughed and went still.

I had done what I came to do, but it didn't make me feel any better. I had kept my promise to Monique that I would find Diana's killer, and I had avenged the erasing of the happy couple's dreams and plans. But I felt as rotten as a dope addict on a down, and I believed I would soon pay for my actions. I left the mess I had made, and headed for a door at the back of the hallway. I needed to breathe fresh air. The door swung outward, and I found myself on the balcony at the rear of the building. Dawn was casting a pink glow across the sky. I headed cautiously toward the sound of gunfire to my right. I turned a corner and stepped into a cross-fire. Pure instinct saved me. I dropped and rolled on the balcony as bullets shredded the railing next to me. Antonio was on open ground to my right and firing in my direction from behind a body he was using as cover. On my left, two black-clad men were firing automatic weapons at him from the opposite corner of the house. They were handicapped by a mist of tear gas that hung around them. The spent grenade lay a few feet from their position. I flipped over a heavy wooden patio table, ducked behind it, and fired. Whether by good aim or good luck—it didn't really matter which—I hit one right between the eyes. He dropped like a poleaxed steer. His partner disappeared around the corner. Antonio gave me a thumbs-up and ran after another terrorist who was taking off on one of the all-terrain trikes.

The slide on one of my pistols was locked open, out of ammo. I dropped the empty magazine, reloaded, and jumped down off the balcony. It wasn't a smart move. I twisted my ankle. I hobbled after Antonio, too slow, too long in the open. Somewhere between the main house and one of huts, the bearded partner of the guy I had shot in the comm room roared up in front of me on one of the balloon-tired ATVs. We both shot and missed at the same time. My pistol stovepiped, jamming partly open. My adversary was close enough to see that I was now helpless. Sliding off his seat, he took a step toward me and, with a mad grin, aimed at my forehead. I dropped the useless weapon as my left hand reached behind my back for my other pistol. I heard snapping sounds from behind him, and he made a face like that of a 5-year-old tasting foul medicine for the first time. In the same second, he seemed to mime my actions, dropping his weapon as he tried to reach behind his back. His head bent forward, his eyes closed, and he dropped to his knees. Close behind him stood another black-clad, hooded man, with a Taser in his hand. The bearded man folded to the ground in slow, jerky movements as the man behind him removed his balaclava to reveal CIA Agent Parks.

I stood frozen in place, uncomprehending.

"You can close your mouth, Beaudry. We put a tracker on your Jeep. Now, you better put your hands on top of your head before you get shot," Parks said.

I complied as more armed men came out of the woods behind him. They wore SWAT team vests with

"POLICE" stenciled on the back and "RCMP-ERT" patches on their shoulders.

"I told you to stay out of this, Beaudry. Now you're in the deep shit," Parks said.

THIRTY-FIVE

I was sitting in the living room of the main house. The handcuffs were off, traded for a guard at my side. Parks talked to his office on a satellite phone as the bearded man and another of his group were led away with looped tie-wraps on their wrists and plastic shackles on their ankles. The bodies of the dead terrorists had been stored temporarily in the basement. Parks appeared to want to clean up the scene and was having problems with the senior officer of the RCMP SWAT team. They argued, both stepping in nose to nose. The SWAT team commander finally lost his cool and threatened to throw Parks out of the country.

From what I overheard, Parks had not been totally honest with Derek, the RCMP SWAT team commander. The morning raid on the camp was supposed to be an easy capture of a bunch of sleepy terrorists in training. Parks had omitted to inform the young officer of the involvement of the Montreal police and that one or more of the terrorists were suspects in an ongoing murder case. Derek was livid at finding a massacre of international dimensions on his hands. He just wanted to get rid of the political hot potato that Parks had dropped in his hands.

Parks finally relented, raised his hands in mock surrender, and walked away from the confrontation. He came to stand next to me and nodded to my guard to move away.

"You're lucky we captured two of the hit team," Parks said. "If you and your partner had killed all of them, I think that I would have shot you myself."

"You're lucky I found them for you," I said. "Let's not get dramatic, all right? We need each other."

"Your partner has disappeared into the woods, but he can't get far. We have officers posted on your Jeep. If we have to, we'll get a K-nine team up here—it's only a matter of time. We have you and a mess of dead bodies, shot or stabbed with some kind of an ice pick. Why would I need anything else?"

Parks had been pacing around the overstuffed chair I was sitting in. He finally calmed down and sat on a couch across from me. While he and Derek were arguing, I had hatched a solution to my dilemma. It was a bit of a reach, but I was sure the CIA had come up with even more outlandish plots.

"Well, first, you need to question the men you captured, and as fast as possible. In your game, old information is like yesterday's stock quotes. You have no police status on this side of the border. I'm sure that you're working with the local authorities strictly on a consulting basis, so you won't be in charge of anything from now on. In Canada, the wheels of justice move slowly and tend to be protective of prisoners until they're actually found guilty. If they were tossed over to your side of the fence, it would make things easier for you and for our politicians. It's not going to look good internationally when it's found out that a small army of terrorists were training under our noses."

"I can't see you being able to toss them over to the U.S," Parks said. "That's not much of a bargaining chip."

"I also know who set up the terrorist-and-banker meeting, and I have proof to back it up."

"I'm still listening, Beaudry."

"The current Quebec government is very touchy about the feds transgressing on their jurisdiction. I saw only RCMP today. I'm sure the local cops don't know about this little quasi-military action. You know I won't go down without a fight. I can make such a stink, you'll be swimming in a river of paperwork molasses for a year. I'm not sure your bosses at Langley will appreciate all the bad publicity you're going to bring them."

"That's all horseshit, Beaudry. You're not in a position to threaten anybody."

I just smiled. You can win a poker game with a good bluff, even if all you've got is a pair of threes. I shook my finger at him as if chiding an unruly child.

"Myself, I would never threaten another officer of the law, even if I had a video of him coming into my apartment, and a taped conversation of him admitting to posing as an employee of the U.S. embassy while actually being a CIA agent—and even if, in that conversation, he were making disparaging remarks about both the CSIS and the Mounties."

Parks stood up and glowered. "You're a real piece of work, Beaudry. I'm sure you can be a thorn in my side and make a mess for us, but your job and future are also in play. I'm curious how you expect to get off the hook and how can you put the terrorists in my hands. And I want the slate cleaned between us."

His blustery attitude couldn't hide the fact that he had folded with a full house to my pair of threes.

"To quote the British judge Gordon Hewart," I said, "'In legal theory and the public view, not only must justice be done; it must also be seen to be done.' In this case, justice has been done, but it would be best for all concerned if nothing seemed to have been done."

"Never mind the monologue, Beaudry—get to the bottom line."

I outlined my plan to Parks and to Derek, the RCMP SWAT team leader. Owing to Derek's animosity toward Parks, he quickly sided with me. My arguments also hit the right note because of the lucky fact that he had shot a doped-up ax-wielding man last year and was still smarting from all the bad publicity.

"I do not need my name on the news again." Derek said. "I'm still in the doghouse with my bosses for an incident last year. We faced a violent young man who was doped up to the eyeballs, he slashed one of the First Nation's police officers and was about to strike one of my trainees. It was a clean shoot, I had no choice. My bad luck that the young addict turned out to be the son of a tribal leader."

An hour or so of give-and-take later, they both nodded in agreement. Parks seemed relieved that the plan had come from me, and he shook my hand, sealing our arrangement. To get back in the good graces of Derek and the RCMP, he volunteered to manage the implementation of my scheme. I had a smile on my face. Not only had they accepted most of my plan, but also, during our negotiations, I had heard the wop-wop of a helicopter coming in, then the roar when it took off minutes later. I surmised that Antonio was safely off to Montreal.

THIRTY-SIX

Like a loaded eighteen-wheeler sliding down a February black-iced overpass, the momentum could no longer be stopped. The big con game that I had set up was rolling inexorably to its denouement. The plan would slide me to safety or send my career crashing through the guardrail in flames. Timing was everything. Each of us had a critical part to play. If an event was out of sequence, the parts of the puzzle would no longer fit together. I used Parks's sat phone to make a few calls. From a friend at City Hall, I found out that the municipal councillor and his bodyguard, Trehearne, were arriving this afternoon on the Air Canada 2:55 flight from Paris. I arranged with the RCMP and customs to intercept them on the walkway as they got off the plane and to hold them for questioning. I had to pick up the incriminating picture of Trehearne from my home safe and then make it to

Trudeau Airport in time to snag him into my game. Even driving well over the speed limit, it was going to be a tight play. Sixty miles from Montreal, my cell phone beeped that I had messages. Driving one-handed, I scrolled to find four missed calls from Pat, one from my boss, Jean, and one from Antonio.

Pat answered on the first ring.

"You called," I said.

"Where are you? I tried to reach you all morning. I wanted you to be the first to know."

"Know what?"

Pat sounded as excited as a teenage girl telling her friends about her great prom date. "Robert, I love being your partner, but I've left homicide. You guys play too rough. I've joined a special squad created to fight corruption in the construction industry and in government. It's a Montreal-based joint task force of local and Quebec City police, provincial police, RCMP, and other agencies. That's what my meeting with Commissioner Martin was all about. He asked me to be a lead investigator in the new anticorruption unit."

I was having a flashback moment of Colleen telling me she was moving to Ottawa for a new job. I said to myself, Shit. What did I not do, to get myself here?

"You seem happy about your new job," I said, "but I'm shocked to hear you're jumping ship. I thought we were getting along fine."

"I told you I wasn't sure about liking homicide but I was sure about you. They're waiting for me for the news conference. I'll call you back, Robert." She said it all in a rush, then hung up.

I wasn't sure whether I had messed up another relationship, this time before it even really began. In my limp hand, the phone buzzed again. I looked at the screen, hoping it was Pat calling back. It was Antonio.

He started talking before I even said hello. "You okay, Beaudry?"

"Yeah, more or less. I developed my own plan B."

"What's the 'less' for?"

"Pat's quit homicide; she's working for another department."

"I knew it, Beaudry. I read you right. You had a thing for her."

"Never mind. Not important. I heard the chopper pick you up. You all in one piece?"

"Somebody trimmed my left eyebrow with a lucky shot," Antonio said, trailing off with a sound somewhere between a chuckle and a growl.

"I'm glad you got to have some fun. I got handcuffed and harassed by the SWAT team. They had a GPS tracking thing on my Jeep."

"How'd you manage to get away? Musta' been some plan B!"

"I used some leverage to convince them it would be best to keep our little raid and theirs a secret."

"What about all the bodies? You buried 'em?"

"Nope, gave 'em away as door prizes. Parks, the CIA guy, has a cleanup-and-disposals team that will strategically place them to fit my plan B. Tomorrow morning, three of them will appear to have been be shot as they tried to cross the Canadian border into the U.S. They'll be armed, and two will be wearing Ghillie camouflage suits. The third will have a backpack full of cocaine. Canada will impress our southern neighbors with our efficiency at stopping drug runners. The RCMP and border patrol will get commendations."

"You're a scoundrel, Beaudry. I love this."

"Three more are killed tonight in an attempted home invasion at a well-known city councillor's mansion. Tomorrow, at JFK in New York, the CIA and U.S. Border Patrol will arrest the two remaining terrorists escorted out of Canada for falsification of entry documents. That takes care of all of them."

"There were nine, not eight, Beaudry. I captured one in the forest. I don't want to bust your bubble and your sneaky plan, but they're not terrorists. When I questioned him, he told me he was part of a team of mercenaries providing twenty-four-seven protection and whatever else for a Mr. Rohmer, a wealthy financier. Two of them left with their German boss earlier this week. The others were to leave in pairs a few days apart to avoid attention."

"Terrorists or mercenaries—at this point in the game, I don't think anybody's going to quibble over semantics. Where's the one you grabbed?"

"He unwisely chose to ride in a helicopter without his seatbelt buckled. Stumbled and fell out."

"Shame," I said. "Safety first, I always say."

"Drop into the restaurant tonight. You sound like you could use a good bottle of Montepulciano. My treat."

"Maybe. I'll call you back."

I called Parks. "I can't tell you my source, but I have intel that our terrorists were not working for El-Rahim. They're bodyguards and assassins for Rohmer, the banker. Two of them left with Rohmer earlier this week. The rest were to leave in pairs during the next few days."

"I'm glad that you're honest enough to tell me, but that's old news, Beaudry. We found that out this morning. And since we're sharing, Mr. Rohmer will no longer be providing funds for terrorists. With a little help from some of our Israeli friends, he suffered an unfortunate boating accident this morning at his estate on Lake Geneva. What goes around . . ."

"Yeah, I've become a believer in that saying. Are you escorting our two remaining mercenaries to New York tomorrow?"

"No, another team's taking over. We have a lead on Rahim. I'm off to Syria. I'll send you a postcard."

"Happy hunting, Parks, I owe you one."

"Someday, I'll pop up on your doorstep. Have a bottle of Famous Grouse on hand. So long, Beaudry."

I didn't call my boss. I needed to meet Trehearne first. My career hung on my ability to convince one of the most straitlaced cops I ever knew, to bend the rules.

THIRTY-SEVEN

At three twenty in the afternoon, traffic on the highway was already bogging down. In an hour, it would be down to a crawl. Springtime predictably brought out green shoots, flowers, and orange construction cones and detour signs throughout Montreal. A Canadian stand-up comic recently quipped that from the orbiting space station, one could see the Great Wall of China and the construction cones of Montreal. I took the next exit and, by rote, followed the service roads and side-street shortcuts to my apartment. I was thinking about Pat and her new job. Though I was loath to admit it, she had made the right decision. She was a good fit for the new investigation team. I couldn't see her staying in homicide, where she would eventually make herself sick over some poor innocent victim. I cared for her, and I would give her my blessing and congratulations on her career choice. I also vowed to take my chances and tell her how I felt.

Nothing risked, nothing gained, I told myself. If I could face flying bullets, I could face the sting of rejection.

But I would let her call back first, and test the water before I dived in.

I parked illegally in the lane behind my house, ran up the back stairs, let Crackers out, cleaned up the cat food spread all over the kitchen floor, got the picture of Trehearne and El-Rahim, and was back on the road inside three minutes.

* * *

I made it to Trudeau Airport twenty minutes late. The arrivals screen displayed flight AC871 as having already landed. I speed-walked to the immigration office, did the badge flip, and explained that I had suspects waiting for me in the holding cells somewhere in the bowels of the airport. A spectacular blonde Valkyrie from Customs escorted me to the elevator, swiped her pass card on the reader, and punched us to a sublevel. She smiled at me; I nodded back and looked down at the floor, my mind in another space, planning what I would say to Pat. I didn't even think of flirting with the voluptuous officer. I was in Pat withdrawal. I had it bad. If my life was a movie, the background music playing would be Bill Withers singing "Ain't No Sunshine." It was a strange feeling to miss her this much. It was as if an earthquake had tilted the ground under me, sliding me toward her, and

I was powerless to do anything about it. Not an earthquake, I supposed, but more of a heartquake. Aside from the staged kiss on our way back from the compound, we had not been physical, yet I missed her like a longtime lover. Working with her as her superior officer, I wasn't allowed to love her, of course. I wasn't supposed to care or to wish she were back beside me, but I couldn't help it. I was smitten.

We made it to the lower floor, where two Customs and Border Service Agency officers and a uniformed Mountie waited for me in an office adjacent to the holding cells.

The senior CBSA officer pulled me aside. "Lieutenant, we detained your suspects because I got confirmation of your request from a CSIS agent that I know. One of the people we detained for you is a police officer; the other claims to be in charge of City Hall. We have no paperwork, warrant, or anything. Their passports are valid, and there's nothing illegal in the luggage. Both of them are having fits and threatening my team with all kinds of lawsuits and political reprisals. I'm not holding them a minute longer if you don't explain real fast what's going on."

I read his name tag. "I appreciate your cooperation, Officer Jankowski," I said, pulling out the photograph of Trehearne and El-Rahim. "If you can make a couple of photocopies of this, it will answer your questions."

He looked at the picture. "This is the police guy that's in holding cell two. Your other man is not the one in this picture. You're not telling me anything with this."

"Scan one of the copies into your database. The man with the goatee will pop out as Hamid El-Rahim, number six on the international Most Wanted Terrorists list. The chubby, arrogant city councillor that you're holding set up a meeting with the terrorist and a crooked Swiss banker to fund another attack on the U.S. or Canada. The other person in the picture, Trehearne, the policeman, is on loan from the mayor as the councillor's bodyguard. He's working undercover with me."

Officer Jankowski stood staring at the picture as if it were growing fangs and about to fold over and bite him.

"Och, mój Boże! This is out of my league. I'll call my boss."

I pulled out my wallet and handed him a business card that Derek, the RCMP SWAT team leader, had given me this morning. "This is the name and number of an RCMP field commander. Call him first, get him down here, and then call your boss. You win more respect for being proactive than reactive," I added with a smile.

Jankowski made the copies and the call. Within twenty minutes, the RCMP-ERT team leader arrived with two other people in tow. He didn't introduce them. They were dressed in civilian clothes but stood at military parade rest. Both said that they were itching to question the city councillor. I headed to holding cell number 2 and a confrontation with my Internal Affairs nemesis, Sergeant Lorne Trehearne.

THIRTY-EIGHT

Jankowski, the customs officer, escorted me to the interrogation room.

"You've got ten minutes, Lieutenant."

He unlocked the door for me and waited outside.

I once told another cop that Lorne Trehearne was a wimp. I was wrong. In today's terms, he's a nerd—a damn smart one. He needs a couple of tries at every shooting range proficiency test, and I wouldn't count on him in a bar fight. But it's said that the pen is mightier than the sword, and to Trehearne's credit, he's a wizard with the spoken and written word. He once nailed a bad cop in our department by analyzing two years of daily reports—not only what was written, but especially what was omitted. It led to Trehearne finding the rotten apple in our midst. He's a desk jockey who drifted into Internal Affairs because nobody wanted the job. And Trehearne didn't much care what anybody thought of him, for most of the street cops had told him they didn't like his meek attitude. Still, I grudgingly must admit that he's good at what he does.

Seeing me walk in, Trehearne jumped out of his chair with a mix of shock, consternation, and disgust on his face, like a mother finding out that her darling son is a pervert.

"Beaudry, what the frig! I can't believe you would go to these lengths to get even with me. I'm not even with Internal Affairs anymore. What the heck is all this bullfeathers about?"

"Trehearne, I can't believe how polite you are, even when you have the right to be angry. I know you're out of Infernal Affairs and working for the mayor. This has nothing to do with your I-A work or getting even with you. In fact, I have to thank you for the suspension. I hadn't realized how troubled I was after Colleen's death. I needed that break to put my head straight. You saw it, and I didn't."

Trehearne, his initial anger vented, flopped down in his seat, rubbing his brow. "I don't understand what you're doing here and why I'm being detained and treated like a criminal."

I took a seat on my side of the table and slid a copy of my incriminating picture across to him. "Who's the guy you're talking to?"

"Prince Khalid Abdulaziz, a wealthy oil magnate."

"I'm afraid not. He's Hamid El-Rahim, number six on the international Most Wanted Terrorists list. Your city councillor boss set up a meeting with Rahim and a crooked banker to bankroll a terrorist operation. You've stumbled into a hornets' nest. The RCMP and CSIS agents are waiting to question you. I've pulled in some favors to talk to you first."

"But I—"

I clasped his forearm and put my finger across my lips. "If you know something about this, you're an accessory to a criminal endeavor. If you know nothing, you're stupid. In either case, even if you get to keep your job, it's not going to make a favorable paragraph on your record."

"So, you're here to gloat, Beaudry. I've dug myself into a hole all by myself. I took the mayor's offer thinking it was a step up, but I found out that I'm just a lowly bodyguard on loan to any of his cronies. Now all this crap may cost me my job and my government pension." Trehearne crumpled the picture into a ball and threw it at me. In a move worthy of Antonio, I caught it in mid flight with my left hand.

"Lorne, you're wrong. I have no animosity toward you. I know you're a good cop. Nobody likes I-A, but somebody has to do the job. I know I bend the rules, and yet, you've always treated me fair."

"I'd like to be treated fairly, also," he whined. "I have nothing to do with this terrorist thing."

"I'm going to help you out of this mess and put a little shine on your record," I said. "However, we have to bend a few rules in the process."

Trehearne shook his head slowly and crossed his arms. "I can't promise anything, but I'll listen. You're the expert on rule bending."

I detailed his role in my play, scene by scene. At the end of my speech, his arms were still crossed but he was leaning forward in his chair—ambiguous body language, to say the least. I didn't let him comment. I brusquely got up and knocked on the door. Derek, the RCMP-SWAT team leader from this morning's raid, walked in, followed by the two men in civilian clothes. I figured they represented other agencies with initials for names.

"Sergeant Trehearne, for now, this meeting is unofficial," Derek said. "We'll dispense with names. I'm RCMP. My colleagues are from INSET and CSIS."

I was going to say I knew it, but refrained doing so. Trehearne stood and nodded politely to the officers.

"Our understanding is that you are working undercover with Lieutenant Beaudry on an investigation into possible links between a City Hall official and a known terrorist. Is that correct?" Derek said.

I was surprised when Trehearne jumped into my game with all the poise of a seasoned Shakespearean actor doing Hamlet.

"Yes, we're working together. I'm acting as a bodyguard for the mayor, and he's been able to place me in the entourage of our main suspect. I have enough notes on file for several counts of criminal activity and dereliction of duty."

"How did you find out about his association with a terrorist?" Derek asked.

"Hamid El-Rahim was posing as Prince Khalid Abdulaziz, a wealthy oil magnate shopping for funding for a new hotel and high-rise condominium complex in Ölüdeniz on the Turkish coast," Trehearne said, his face deadly serious. "From what I overheard between the banker Rohmer and the supposed prince, it didn't feel right. The money transfers were to be sent via Pakistan. That rang alarms for me, so I sent a picture of Rohmer, the prince, and myself to Beaudry for him to verify the identities of both Rohmer and Khalid."

"Good work," said the nameless CSIS officer.

Trehearne smiled. "We still have a few pieces of the puzzle to put together, and I have to report to the mayor."

Derek, playing his part, closed the deal. "We're going to hang on to the city councillor; he seems to want to cooperate. When we're finished with him, you can have him back. Pick him up at our HQ in Westmount tomorrow morning. Now, both of you get out of here and make sure to get all your paperwork in order."

"Come on, buddy, you did a good job," I said. "Let's wrap this up."

I grabbed Trehearne by the arm and led him out. Through my fingertips, I could feel him tremble.

THIRTY-NINE

We were back in traffic and headed for the city councillor's house.

Trehearne was in the passenger seat, his luggage in the back of my Jeep.

"I don't like taking credit for something I didn't do," he said. "I'm not at ease with your plan, Beaudry, particularly the second part."

"Look, Lorne," I said, "I know that you don't like bending rules. But there are no rules in love or war, and the free world is at war against the terrorists. They use indiscriminate violence that has nothing to do with fair play or written procedures. If we want to stop another Nine-eleven, we just have to act as best we can."

We stopped at a red light, and a vagrant holding a sign that read 'No Job No Food- Can You help' came winding between the lines of waiting cars. Trehearne wiggled in his seat, fishing in his pockets, slid down his window, and handed the man some coins. The man gave a nod of mild gratitude, and Trehearne pressed the up button on the armrest.

Turning to me as if nothing had happened, he said, "You think what we're doing will count?"

"I don't know for sure. What I do know is that Rahim was looking for funds—and not to open a day-care center. The CIA agents told me their informants warned that an important terrorist attack against the West was in the works and that some of Rahim's old group were mobilizing. But they never found out what was targeted. Yes, we're bending rules today, but we may be saving thousands of lives. Counterintelligence actions are secret; nobody will ever know how close we came to another disaster."

"I'm not comfortable, but I have to admit that a terrorist bomb has no rules of engagement in the blast zone—it kills anybody: women, children, whoever. Nonetheless, it doesn't mean all of our rules have to go out the door."

"Lorne, let's just take it a step at a time," I said.

I'd seen acrobats in Old Montreal with less balancing skills than Trehearne. I gave him my best sales pitch, and he was still on the fence.

We were passing a burger joint when Trehearne said, "I feel faint. All I got today was a little airplane meal. They didn't even give me coffee in the holding cell."

I nodded. "I'm always hungry. All I ate was a sandwich early this morning. There's no rush; we have time for a bite."

I turned the Jeep into the restaurant parking lot.

We had just started our meal when my phone rang. It showed Pat's number. I slid out of the booth with my triple burger, saying, "I have to take this call. Enjoy your salad. Take your time. I'll be outside."

I put the phone to my ear and said, "I'm glad you phoned back."

"Sorry it took so long," she said. "It's been a media circus all day. I was hoping I could see you tonight."

"Rats, and double rats."

"What?"

"No, no. I mean, that would be wonderful. I said 'rats' because I'm stuck with something for a good few hours."

"That's okay, Robert. It'll give me time to change. Call me when you're free."

"I thought of you all day," I said. "I have to tell you that that you made the right choice. Homicide's not for you. You'll do a great job in investigations. It didn't shape up like I'd hoped, but that's life, I guess."

"Thanks for your confidence in my abilities, but I don't understand the last part you just said."

With my free hand, I turned up my collar against the evening chill. I backed up against the building, shielding myself against the wind and, perhaps subconsciously, against a potential rejection.

"Pat, I'm not a man of many words. It's just that I'll miss you . . . a lot."

"Miss me? What are you talking about, you muppet of a bear? I told you I loved being your partner. I wasn't sure about liking homicide, but I was sure about you. You weren't listening to what I wasn't saying at all, at all. And yourself a great detective, now."

"Well, yesterday you felt very distant. I didn't know what to think."

"Robert, you big handsome lug, I fought me urges every day to resist the werebear, or we would both of us been in trouble. Uncle Jean woulda' suspended ya faster than an old maid trying to catch the bridal bouquet."

"I can't tell you how happy that makes me," I said.

"Being suspended?"

"No, you silly redhead—the other part."

"Ah, we're on the same page now. I'll see you later at your place. I still have your apartment key . . . and we're no longer in the same department, ya know." Pat hung up with the sound of a kiss.

Good thing I was still hanging on to my weighty triple burger, or else I might have floated off the ground.

Trehearne came out the door with a perplexed frown. "What's that silly grin, Beaudry? Something funny?"

"It's a long story. Let's get back on the road."

We got in the Jeep and headed for the final scene of my little play.

FORTY

Arriving at the councillor's house, I spotted the black Humvee parked across the street. Parks's gray Buick, or an exact replica, took up the last space on the street. I backed the Jeep into the driveway, setting up for a fast escape.

A tall, gaunt man, wearing the same nondescript gray suit that CIA agents seemed to favor, met us at the door. His face looked long and terribly sad, like that of a mortuary attendant in a play.

"Good evening, Mr. Tremont," he whispered as he handed Trehearne a key in a small plastic bag.

"Trehearne," Lorne replied as he unlocked the front door.

Another gray-clad man waited for us in the hallway inside. This shorter one looked strong and agile, with the solid build of a running back.

"You guys all use the same tailor?" I said.

The running back said, "Difficult color to remember—changes depending on the lighting. It can be anything from light blue to dark brown."

I nodded. "I learn something every day."

He asked Trehearne to turn on the light and open the pocket door to the living room.

The spooks had done a masterful job. The walls behind us had a few bullet holes, a coffee table just a little out of place, a pillowcase of valuables dropped on the floor. I noted that all the supposed perpetrators of the home invasion were now in civilian clothes. I recognized Antonio's first victim. His body was slumped in a living-room chair as if he had fallen backward from a standing position. Two other bodies were sprawled in the doorway between this room and the dining room.

"You guys should get an Oscar for set design," I said. "This looks just right."

"Thank you," Running Back replied. "Few people appreciate the care needed in cleanup and disposals."

The agent with the mortician's face pointed to the corpse in the chair. "This one was difficult: He got stabbed with some kind of ice pick. We had to insert a fired bullet precisely into the same wound cavity."

I pointed to the bullet hole. "Do you think this'll fool the coroner?"

I didn't think it possible, but he took on an even sadder demeanor and shook his head.

"No, this is just for show at the scene. We have a paperwork snafu in the works. The bodies will be inadvertently transferred to Ontario. We have another team working on sending them to the right pathologist. By the time all is sorted out, well, you know . . ." He tilted his head to the side.

We formed a semicircle around the body, discussing its positioning as if it were just another piece of furniture in the room.

Trehearne's jaw clenched as the running back handed him one of my CZ-85 pistols they had confiscated at the camp this morning.

With gloved hands, they took the body out of the chair and held it up in a standing position.

Trehearne was ashen. "You have to put one in his chest," I said.

With a shaking hand, he aimed the gun. I was afraid he would shoot one of the spooks. They were pulling to the side, like the two Dallas cops escorting Lee Harvey Oswald when Jack Ruby shot him. I put on my blue surgical gloves and held his wrist for him. Trehearne closed his eyes and pulled the trigger.

They repositioned the body in the chair. "Perfect," the mortuary man said. "The others are done. The fingerprints are where we want them, and he has gunshot residue on his hand. The rented Buick in front is from the airport. We used Tremont's credit card number. I think our work is done."

"Trehearne," Lorne corrected again. "Beaudry, I still don't like this one bit."

The running back stepped up to save the play. "Mr. Trehearne, you are doing a great service to both our countries. These men were dangerous killers for hire to terrorists or anybody else with a criminal plan, but they were unknown to most law enforcement agencies. Now they will be out of action, no longer available for terrorist activities. We've fabricated criminal records in your central database. Now they're part of a Toronto gang, each with a lengthy rap sheet. Tomorrow morning, a captain from Metro Toronto's anti-gang squad will call your mayor, commending your good work. There's too much at stake here for second-guessing. We appreciate your bravery, and we owe you a debt of gratitude."

Trehearne puffed up a little, nodding politely. "Thank you, Officer."

Mr. Undertaker gave his last whispered commands. "We will exit from the kitchen and fire the appropriate number of blank shots so that your story may be corroborated by neighbors. Use that phone to call nine-one-one. Good luck, Mr. Trehearne, and thank you again."

"I'll move the Jeep down the street," I said. "I prefer not to be on the scene, but if you're really stuck, call me and I'll come back."

"Beaudry, I'm still not sure if I should kiss you or kick you in the groin. Get out of here. I'll be okay."

I gave him a light buddy punch on the shoulder. "Neither option is appealing," I said. "I'm hoping you can find some middle ground. Now, go get 'em, tiger." And I gave him a crisp salute.

FORTY-ONE

I parked one street over, parallel to the councillor's house. I could view his driveway from between buildings. Within a few minutes, three police cars had arrived: code one upgrade, lights but no sirens. Five minutes later, a supervisor's van parked in the driveway. I waited half an hour. There was no emergency call from Trehearne. I wished I had hidden a camera in the house so I could see the show. Based on his performance in the airport holding cell, I was sure he could pull it off and earn himself a commendation in the process.

He would owe me a favor for my making him look the hero, but I knew he wouldn't give me an inch of leeway if he ever caught me bending the rules again.

I vowed not to get caught. Some of Pat's lucky charm must have rubbed off on me. Diana's killers had been disposed of; I had inherited a new and trustworthy friend, even if he was a criminal; by all appearances, I never fired a shot; and as far as I knew, I was still in my boss's good graces. More importantly, I was going home to Pat. I was one lucky cop. I was on the road home, impatient at the slow evening traffic and at every forced stop. I seemed to be catching every single red light, and I was sure they had added more stop signs on this road.

I finally arrived at my street. Pat's Mustang was parked across from my condo. I jumped out of my car and rushed to the stairs. Halfway up to the balcony, I missed a step and had to grab the handrail to avert a fall. My sore ankle complained about my jogging up the stairs. I fumbled with my key but finally got my front door open.

My Bose sound system was playing soft jazz, and the lighting was dimmed low. In the living room, a trail of unrolled toilet paper led down the hall to form an arrow pointing to the kitchen. I smiled. Pat had taken a play from Crackers, it seemed.

On my kitchen table, an ice bucket held a bottle of Prosecco bubbly wine. The plates were set for two around a tall unlit pink candle. A handwritten note leaned against the base of the candlestick. "Don't peek in the fridge. I ordered a fancy meal from your favorite restaurant. First, we have dessert." It was signed with a red sticker in the shape of a woman's lips.

I had a feeling I was about to owe Antonio for his two-hundred-dollar bet.

I stepped back into the hallway. "Where are you, Pat?"

"I'm in the bedroom, waiting for the werebear."

I got there as gracefully as I could. Pat was in my king-size bed, the sheet pulled up to her neck. She wasn't wearing her special titanium-melting smile. This one was more subtle and coy.

I cleared my throat. "I'll bet you're naked under that sheet."

She dropped the sheet. "You win."

###

MICHAEL KENT is an international management and coaching consultant. Contrary to his technical writing, his fiction always has tinge of humor and a special twist to the tale.

A native of Montreal, he is fully bilingual, normally in the same sentence. Years as a private pilot, avid reading and extensive traveling, have generated a storehouse of plots and stories that still have to be shared with the world. A member of Canadian Crime Writers, he is also active with Writers on the net, Writers Village University and The Next Big Writer.

http://www.kent-writer.com/

The Lieutenant Beaudry series :

Blood tail
Folded dreams
Twice dead
Voodoo Dead

43268972R00138

Made in the USA
Lexington, KY
27 July 2015